I0571559

BRASH FLOW

**A NOVELLA
IN 17 TRACKS**

PATRICK HOLM

For Lucille, Josephine, and Florence.
You're the future.

"It's yours! The world in the palm of your hand."
—WU-TANG CLAN

BRASH FLOW

TRACK 1

JOHN HENRY WAS SEARCHING FOR two things. The first thing he was pretty sure existed. It was a piece of electronics. The second thing was a different story.

It had been a couple of months since he had taken apart an eshirt. He found the communication center that took what the advertiser said and flashed the ad on the front and back of the shirt. It looked like old technology from earlier in the century. They probably still used it because that's what they had used when they first created it and never bothered upgrading it. He thought he might be able to send his own messages to the shirt if he could find the right part. There was even a chance he might be able to control the eshirts around him.

Eshirts had been around longer than he had. The credits you could earn from wearing an eshirt made it the default fashion. People were looking for easy ways to supplement their income. Internet ads had expanded to shirts. Unavoidable pop ups walking everywhere. Outfits became a full time walking commercial, scrolling from one to the other. Eshirts had sound for a period but it was dropped after a few tragic deaths at a subway stop.

Social media and eshirts were made for each other. Everyone received similar baseline contracts with the ad agencies to start with. If the wearers social media stock shot up from celebrity status or a viral web video, they could try and renegotiate their contract. Bottom floor eshirt money was not much. It did help with the small things though. More feed for your 3D. More food options in your insta. Everyone did it. Everyone who could.

The Flip came in 2037. Within a couple of months, the environment and atmosphere reached a tipping point and deteriorated exponentially like experts had warned. Droughts and dust bowls. Hurricanes and floods. Heat waves and cold fronts. The most notable change though, was the increase in solar radiation. Before everyone knew what happened the majority of the fair skinned population was toast, seas of burnt corpses. Most people of color had just enough pigment to dodge these solar death rays. There were some folks on the edges that made it and some that didn't, but the sun largely discriminated by race. It left the world with Whites and Blacks.

Once the Flip happened, the Pigeon Code denied Whites the right to wear eshirts. The only thing they could wear were their Solar Mitigation and Resistance Kits, SMiRK for short. It was a white suit with a hood that covered your entire body and shielded it from solar radiation. It wasn't that Whites were legally bound to wear the SMiRK, but there weren't many other options when the sun's rays led to instant death. Messing with the eshirts was illegal. Corporations and advertising agencies wanted full control.

John Henry was aware of the risk he was taking by just having the eshirt. But messing with it? That took it to another level. He would be breaking multiple Pigeon Code ordinances and could go to jail for a long time.

The second thing he was searching for was what made it worth it. He was searching for the perfect beat, the perfect flow. Trying to put together the perfect combination of rhymes. Create the show that would put him on the map as a rapper, to get those emcee credits. Get his mom out of the Wrash. He would daydream. The sky was the limit. Flipping words in his heads. Tapping beats on machines and nearby objects. If he could use the eshirts to bust on the scene, he didn't see it as a risk. It was the only way.

John Henry heard about Guru's at the last show he had been to. Some people in the audience were talking about how they found an old hip hop album at this weird junk electronic store. John Henry was always on the prowl for new old music. He looked up the place and realized it was a mix between a pawn shop, electronics repair shop, and vintage record store.

Guru's was the perfect place to search for both things. The location of Guru's gave him pause. It was deep on the Black side of town and way past the Pigeon Line. Going there, even during the daytime, was technically illegal. The subway ran close, but he would have to walk four blocks to Guru's from the station.

He grabbed his backpack and headed out. It was late morning, so he would have time to make it to Guru's and back before curfew took effect. There were only a few subway stations going out of Wrashtown. Whites with jobs outside of the Wrash funneled through these stations. Whites frequented the subway to stay out of the sun, even with their SMiRK on, as a general precaution. Plus, walking the streets always invited random police stops.

John Henry looked at his watch just after he scanned through the subway gate. Enough credits to get back and buy his electronics if he found them. He would have to fix something for someone to get his balance back up. The first of the month was a couple of weeks out and he and his mom would have to eat.

He looked around for a seat, but there were no spots. He pushed pass some people standing near the doors and grabbed a strap in the corner. He tapped his watch and put on some music to zone out and hype himself up for the four-block walk. The subway car lurched and started to go.

Seats freed up as the subway made its way across town. John Henry stayed standing. A few Blacks got on after the subway passed the Pigeon Line. They stood in front of several Whites. Their eshirts reflected off the interior of the subway car and most notably the SMiRKs of the Whites sitting in front of them. One of the Blacks gave a flick of the wrist and the Whites lowered their heads and stood up for them to sit. John Henry lowered his head too as did most of the remaining Whites in the subway car. A communal acquiesce born out of fear.

John Henry tapped his foot to the beat of his music and looked up at the subway map. There were four stops to go. His nerves started to build, and he switched the song to something faster to match his heartbeat. This was the first time he had traveled this deep across town without a work order. He could get arrested if the police stopped him.

Sometimes the Pigeon Police would hang out at the exits of the subway lines this side of the Pigeon Line to harass Whites. His plan was to keep his head down and not make eye contact with anyone. He clenched his backpack straps as he stepped off the subway car. He looked both ways for police and headed to the escalator.

He couldn't tell if it was the bass in his headphones or his heart driving through his body. The sweat on his forehead made the SMiRK stick and feel clammier than usual. There were not many people in the White line station. He took the stairs one step at a time with his head down. He felt the warmth of the sun play on his SMiRK and gave a quick glance around at the street. He didn't see any police, just people going about their business.

The nearest person gave his SMiRK a sideways glance, but then kept walking. He did the same and headed the direction of Guru's.

He crossed the last street and found himself standing in front of the door to Guru's. There were no police along the route. He figured he was so far past the Pigeon Line that police patrols were probably more intermittent than near the White side of town. He hesitated to grab the door and go in. The thought that this might be the place where he found what he needed made his skin prickle. The other thought that did not cross his mind until right then is what he would say to Guru on why he was there. He swallowed and walked in.

As the door closed behind him, he stopped and looked around. He didn't see anybody but surveyed the store. In front of him were rows of tables with crates. The crates immediately in front of him had large records in them, to his left looked like smaller records, and to his right there was a display case with some of the large and small records and various other items. Beyond the crates there were aisles that extend back, but he couldn't see the back of the store.

"Boy, what are you doing with that SMiRK on in my store?" a voice said from John Henry's right.

John Henry jumped and looked up. He scanned to find the voice. He found the owner sitting on a stool behind the display case. It looked like he had one of the small records in his hands.

"Excuse me sir?" John Henry managed to spit out. All the nerves that had left him upon getting to the store came rushing back. This man could call the police, something he hadn't thought about in his daydream of finding his electronics.

"I said what are you doing with that SMiRK on in my store," the man repeated, interrupting John Henry's thoughts. "Take it off boy."

"But…" John Henry started to say.

"Look, you're inside. You're fine. There are no windows. Take the fucking thing off. I can't have customers coming in here seeing a SMiRK digging in the crates," the man said with a tone that left no room for question. It was either that or leave the store.

"Okay," John mumbled. Relaxing a little as he realized the man had no intention of calling the police. Maybe kick him out of the store but that he could deal with.

It took him a couple of minutes to work through all of the straps and seals of the SMiRK and gather the hood, suit, and gloves. It formed an awkward bundle under his arm.

"Dark-skinned, huh?" the man asked. "I guess I always picture a white skinned cracker under those things. You want to set that down behind the counter until you leave?"

He was referring to John Henry's darker skin, which was not much lighter than the man's skin. The man's tone sounded almost friendly. The main thing that separated Whites and Blacks was wearing a SMiRK. John Henry did it because his mom had to. Otherwise he could pass as Black with his SMiRK off.

"So, what are you doing here boy?" the man asked with a smile. John Henry wasn't sure if it was because he had his SMiRK off or that the man realized he was dark-skinned. Maybe it was both.

"I heard you had electronics and music," John Henry said. "I'm looking for phones from around 2020 and I'm always looking for good music."

"Electronics are in the back. Follow me," said the man as he stood up. John Henry realized by the man's slow gait that he was older than he looked. "I doubt you'll find any good music in here. I don't keep much of what's out these days."

"Are you Guru?" John Henry asked.

The man chuckled.

"No, I just took that name from one of my favorites. My name is Gibran."

Gibran opened a door to the back. It had more of a warehouse feel than the front, with concrete floors and a work bench with tools along the front wall. Towards the back there were crates, boxes, and shelves brimming with scrap electronics. John Henry stared at everything in wonder. He fixed electronics to earn credits, so he was used to them, but this was different. He had never seen so many in one place.

"Feel free to look as long as you want. I'll be up front," Gibran said.

John Henry nodded his head and walked forward unsure of where to start. The door shut behind Gibran. John Henry glanced back still wondering if Gibran would call the police. He was distracted from that thought when he saw an 808 drum machine sticking out of a crate amongst some other electronics. He pulled it out of the crate and set it on the work bench. The one he had in his apartment was a lot more beat up and he had spent months repairing it. He had better tools to make beats but fixing up the drum machine made him feel like he had bridged a connection with the pioneers of hip hop. As if he had unlocked the secrets of the past. He thumbed the knobs and let his fingers dance over the bottom row of buttons creating imaginary beats.

At that moment, someone walked through the door. It wasn't Gibran, instead a stranger looked at him, nodded his head, and walked into the maze of shelves. John Henry hadn't realized he was holding his breath and let it out. He was primed for a racially charged interaction but remembered between his dark skin and the SMiRK off, the man had no reason to suspect he was White.

This lack of interaction made John Henry a little lightheaded. It made him wonder how easy life would be if he could walk with the SMiRK off and not worry about being harassed by the police or anybody else. He left the drum machine on the work bench and headed into the shelves himself, more determined than ever to find the phones.

* * *

He had been looking for two hours one crate at a time. He managed to find another 808 machine, new headphones, and some cables he could use, but no phones. He hadn't even made it down one side of the aisle. This could take him months, years if he was only able to sneak over to this side of town every couple of weeks. The thought of this squeezed his stomach tight.

"What if there weren't even any phones here?" he thought to himself.

He picked up his backpack and grabbed the headphones and cables. He headed up front. When he was back in the front, he heard the beginning of a song from the late 1990s by Binary Star. He recognized the intro sample of Bruce Lee. The song was Honest Expression.

"Gibran, I thought you said you didn't have any good music? This track is dope." John Henry testing out a little codeswitching as he lay what he found on the counter.

"What do you know about this song, boy? Don't bullshit me. You ain't never heard this song before." Gibran clapped back but didn't chastise him on his familiar tone.

" 'I ain't hardcore, I don't pack a 9-millimeter, most of y'all gangsta rappers ain't hardcore neither', " John Henry rhymed in line with song.

Gibran looked at him and started cracking up.

"Where the fuck did that come from? Shit, I don't even want to know. But respect. This record blew my mind when it first came out. What else do you got?" Gibran followed up.

"Try me."

" 'I take seven emcees put 'em in a line, and add seven more brothers who think they can rhyme', " Gibran rattled off without hesitation.

"Rakim the God," John Henry.

" 'I'm like the fly Malcolm X, buy any jeans necessary', " Gibran went again.

"That's Kan the Louis Vuitton Don," John Henry quipped back. "You going easy on me Gibran?"

Gibran thought for a second.

" 'I once ate a plate made of 88 steaks and you wanted beef? I guess that's the breaks', " Gibran rhymed with a smile on his face.

John Henry's face scrunched in thought.

"Kurtis Blow?" he said without confidence.

"Aww, I got you there. Living Legends, Bicasso. Impressed you know Kurtis Blow though." Gibran said chuckling to himself. "I'll give it to you. You know some hip hop. You find what you were looking for?"

"Nah, but I did find these headphones and cables that I can probably use. You got some cool shit back there. I found an 808 that puts my fixed-up Frankenstein setup to shame."

"When you comin' back again?" asked Gibran.

"I don't know," said John Henry. "I risked getting arrested by the cops and harassed by Blacks just to get here today. Not something I want to do on a regular basis."

"Why would they arrest you?" Gibran asked.

"Do they even need a reason?" John Henry replied. "But mainly because I'm past the Pigeon Line without a work visa."

"Aww no work visa. That's why you were so nervous when you came in here. How about this? I'll hire you and sign off on a work visa. You can keep coming to look for whatever you're trying to find, but we gotta talk hip hop. I haven't met anyone in years who knew Binary Star let alone could rap the lyrics. You'll have to fix stuff for me too. Nothing for free. I got all kinds of broken shit back there. Definitely more valuable if they work."

John Henry thought about it. The police were still going to stop him. It was inevitable. The work visa would at least let him off. A work visa wouldn't stop Blacks from harassing him though. He would just have to watch his back. Whites don't get mirked like they used to, but the streams still talked about it here and there.

The upside was he would have unlimited access to the electronics in the back. That could narrow his search time down to weeks. He didn't get many opportunities to talk hip hop or find new music and this place could do both. And of course, he would be able to pass some more credits to his mom for rent and food.

"I'm in. Let's do it."

A few minutes later Gibran wrapped up going through a few quick prompts on his device. To conclude, he scanned John Henry's watch device to upload the visa. John Henry was good to go.

John Henry was back in his SMiRK and getting ready to head out the front, when Gibran called out.

"John Henry. Don't even think about walking out that way with your SMiRK on. Go through the back. That's the way you should come in to. Don't forget to take the SMiRK off before you come up front when you're back either. Peace."

"Peace out," John Henry acknowledged as he headed to the back of the store.

TRACK 2

THE HARSH FLASHING OF ESHIRTS made it dizzying to try and focus on a face in the crowd. Stilletta James cut through the kaleidoscope. Her skin was dark and movements fluid but what separated her was her dark shirt. No lights, no LEDs. No blinking message or video. She was a moving blackhole among the exploding stars. Drawing all of their light and attention in as she walked and reflecting none. A focused pupil, searching for something. She turned into a building and the lights swallowed up the negative comet.

The system of the building she was in muted the eshirts bringing her a little closer to earth. She headed straight for the elevator tubes without hesitation. Not acknowledging anyone or anything around her. She pressed the button and waited. One of the elevators to her left opened. She made a step toward the doors then stopped as a SMiRK clad worker hustled around the corner and into the elevator. She stepped back. Her brows furrowed, and her lips pursed. She looked at her watch and pressed the button again once the first elevator closed. She grabbed the next elevator up.

She exited on the tenth floor and made her way to down the hall. The door slid open as Stilletta walked in. The receptionist was just a few steps from the door. The screen lit up as it recognized her presence.

"Welcome," the screen displayed. "Please confirm your identity."

The screen requested her to enter her identification number. She entered the ten characters with the speed of regular use. The rote muscle memory that guides the body through tasks it would take the active mind longer to think about.

The receptionist then prompted her to put her hand on the screen and look into the camera.

"Henrietta James, Identity confirmed," displayed the receptionist. Her watch lit up simultaneously checking her in. "Please wait until your name is called. Tap screen to end session."

Stilletta James tapped the screen as she turned around and it went dark. There were six chairs in the waiting room. Three of them were taken. By the unfocused look in their eyes, Stilletta assumed they were all engaged with their Ox. She looked at one of the waiters and then to the empty seats. She walked to the corner opposite the door and stood with one foot against the wall. There were no windows, but she turned her head toward the wall and looked as if she were studying a landscape. Stilletta pulled up her headphones and tapped her watch. She hated using the Ox and preferred to lose herself in the music instead.

The receptionist cycled through the people in the room until it came to her.

"Henrietta James," the receptionist called out. The voice repeated in her headphones as well.

Henrietta pushed off her foot and walked deeper into the building. She paid no attention to the watch direction prompts as she made her way down the hall.

"Henrietta, you're back! It's been a week! I thought you would have come sooner. It's not your steeze to take so long."

The owner of the voice was wearing an angular navy pinstripe suit. His hair was slicked back and reflected the light. His hand extended out to shake Stilletta's. His watch device was plated in real gold contrasting against his fake smile.

"Stilletta, Frank," she said with edge in her voice ignoring his hand.

"Who am I to go against your god given name?" he responded sarcastically.

"Fuck you Frank, you don't know me."

"Easy Henri....Stilletta," Frank said. Fake smile beaming. "What do you want from me?" He stressed the word want to remind her she was here to see him.

"You know why I'm here. My last show sold out. Heads outside had to stream it on their Ox. Through *your* company's service. I killed it. What's up with my credit situation? How much are you bumping me?"

Frank grabbed his device on the table and touched the screen as if he was calculating. It was hard to tell if he was putting on a show or coming up with real numbers.

"I can bump you up 50 credits a month."

"50 fucking credits? Are you serious? You're wrashing me. The Hive holds a couple thousand people. You made at least 10 credits a head."

"Hey, this is what I can offer. Company rules."

"That's bullshit. Doomsday can't even sell the Hive out, let alone get streaming money and ya'll are giving him double what I get."

"I can't discuss Doomsday's deal with you. Part of his contract. Company rules again."

"Like you even need to. Doomsday is always popping his mouth off about his contract."

"Have you ever thought about joining up with Doomsday? He's got good name recognition. It would be a split, but you would still get a bump. And company policy might get you farther that way." The company policy he was referring to was men getting paid more than women. It was 2062 and nothing had changed.

"Me and Doomsday?" scoffed Stilletta James. "Fuck that! Doomsday is garbage. Repping his gold collar like he's somebody. He ain't shit. Wrash motherfucker couldn't spit a decent rhyme if he was about to get mirked."

"How about this?" Frank said as he straightened his collar and slicked back his hair. "I can give you a bonus of 100 credits."

"I don't want your pity money. I want the real money. I need the monthly bump," Stilletta denied him. In her head she knew turning down 100 credits was foolish. All she could think of was Doomsday checking his watch and seeing his credits go up. That thought left no room for retreat in her mind.

"Whoa, whoa, easy," the credit agent said. "You know how we make our money. Entry and streaming are nothing."

"I'm not doing an eshirt."

"Why not? Your stream game is brash. You wouldn't need to sign that many deals to get a good bump."

"Of course, that's what you want. You're making a gang of credits every time someone signs a new deal. My bump would pale in comparison to what you would get. Look at your damn watch. That's a drug dealer watch. You push this on people and then make it right back when you get them to sign contracts for streaming."

"Hey, that's their choice. I don't force it on anyone."

"Yeah right," Stilletta rolled her eyes. "You would sell an eshirt to a smirk if you thought you could get away with it."

Frank laughed.

"It looks like you got our system down. You know how we operate," he said maintaining his snarky tone. "Maybe you should just come and get a job with us."

"Please and be a fucking dealer? Y'all leeches and don't care about shit."

"Probably for the best. If your selling skills were anything like your rapping you would be living in Wrashtown," Frank snorted in derision.

Stilletta's nostrils flared and her eyes grew wide. She picked up his device and threw it at the wall and stormed out. The screen cracked and went dark as it fell to the ground.

"I'm taking that out of your next month," Frank yelled out the door.

Stilletta pounded the wall as she walked down the hallway. The conversation had not gone how she planned. Now she needed to figure out how to get back the credits she just lost.

"Thanks for coming Henrietta," the receptionist said as she walked across the waiting room, interrupting her thoughts.

TRACK 3

IT HAD BEEN A WEEK since John Henry had gone to Guru's. He wanted to go back the very next day, but his credit situation kept him home. Salary was the one thing he didn't discuss with Gibran before he headed out. It had crossed his mind at the time, but he didn't want to press his luck after Gibran gave him the work visa. If he was going to make it back there and continue his search for the electronics, he was going to have to ask for a salary.

John Henry had found someone three units over who needed their 3D fixed. He tried to stick to things he liked to repair, like watches, headphones, and Ox's, but he needed to get back to Guru's. The 3D repair gave him enough to head back and with a little extra left over for food money.

The subway was a lot less stressful this time. Having the work visa meant he had papers. If he was harassed by the police, it wouldn't get him out of trouble but at least he wouldn't be arrested.

John Henry felt like the subway was a cell in a body getting carried down the bloodstream. As he got in the car he put on Black Star's "Respiration." John Henry pictured his breath synchronized with the City's rhythm and melted inward.

The car pulled to a stop and John Henry walked out on to the platform. He pulled his headphones down to his neck. He took a deep breath and the thick dank air of the tunnel coated his throat. Normally, the feeling made him a little queasy, but with the visa in his pocket it felt refreshing. He almost had a bounce in his step as he headed onto the street.

John Henry was walking to Guru's on cruise control. His headphones were still down, and his Ox was off as he floated down the sidewalk. The piles of electronics in the back of Guru's occupied his mind. How many more bins and stacks would he have to work through to find the phone he needed? Was it even there? He decided if it was going to be anywhere, it was going to be there. It was his only hope.

"Hey smirk, where do you think you're going?" a voice interrupted his thoughts.

John Henry turned around and saw two police officers. He knew they were Pigeon Police by their grey uniforms. His body stiffened, and his stomach clenched. He inhaled the hot air through his SMiRK mask, and it formed an oppressive lump in his throat as he swallowed it.

"Did you hear me smirk? I said, where are you going?" the older of the two officers repeated. The deep furrow in his brow and the husky edge in his voice conveyed he had been at this a long time.

John Henry felt the weight of both sets of eyes pressing on him and knew he had made a mistake. He hadn't broken a law, but the visa in his pocket had made him feel invincible. The hardness in the officer's voice shattered this illusion in an instant.

"I...I...have a visa," John Henry said as he reached for his pocket.

"Don't move!" the younger officer shouted at him as he pulled out his gun. "Get your hands up!"

John Henry's arms froze. Not sure if he should freeze or if he should put his hands up. It felt like either movement could get him shot. He read reports like this all of the time. He never knew how he should react, and he still didn't.

"I said get your fucking hands up!"

He decided to go with moving his hands. He closed his eyes and could feel the sweat beading up on his face under his mask. His heart was no longer in sync with the city. It was pumping out of his chest. He moved his hands. He lifted them inch by inch trying to remember to breath as he did it.

"I'll ask you again. Where are you going?"

"I'm headed to Guru's," John Henry forced out. "I have a visa. It's in my pocket."

The younger officer moved forward. He kept one hand on his gun and reached for John Henry with the other. He jostled John Henry as he looked for the pocket. He fumbled and pulled the visa out with the one hand. He held it up to the eye with his Ox and scanned the document. After that, he pulled John Henry's wrist down by his watch device. He holstered his gun and tapped his own watch device and held it next to John Henry's. His gave a bright green flash.

"He checks out," the younger officer said. The disappointment in his voice was clear. John Henry let out the breath he was holding, and his body loosened just a little bit.

The older officer took the visa from his partner.

"Visa or not. I don't like seeing a smirk on these streets. If we catch you out here after curfew, we'll arrest you on the spot. You can forget about that visa too. But between you and me, if we catch you, you'll be lucky. I can't say the same for others. Haven't seen anybody mirked in a long time, but then again, I haven't seen a smirk in a while either. You figure it out."

He handed the visa back to John Henry. They turned and walked off.

John Henry stood still on the sidewalk with the visa in hand. His breathing became regular and he regained control of his heartbeat. He turned and headed to Guru's.

He scanned his watch against the backdoor lock wondering if it would work. He heard a click and pulled the door open to enter the back warehouse of Guru's. When the door shut behind him, the tension in his body from the police stop and frisk finally released. A hollow ache took its place. The piles of electronics chilled him out further. He welcomed Gibran's no SMiRK rule. Shedding the suit put his skin in contact with the fresh air and he felt like he was a real human again.

John Henry felt the call of the bins around him, but he wanted to check in up front with Gibran. Plus, he had been thinking of their last interactions and wondering what hip hop groups he could bring up to impress Gibran.

"My man, Johnny Steel. What's good?"

"Steady old king, even breathin'."

"Shit boy, you don't look steady. Who spookin' you?"

"You can tell? Shit…Pigeon Pats shook me down just now. Iron out and all. Right in my grill."

"You push back?" Gibran asked as he raised his eyebrow.

"Nah king, I was just walking. Straight up," John Henry said and then told him the rest of the story.

"Well shit, you're deep past the Pigeon Line. I guess you're gonna have to keep your head up and move slow. Especially those hands boy. You better keep them out your pockets. They'll shoot you and nobody will ask questions. The young Pats are always ready to pop off, but the old ones have some deep-seated anger. They're the ones to really watch out for."

"What you mean king?"

"Some of those guys have been around since before the Flip. They remember what shit used to be like. When they got the gun pointed in their face for nothin'. When a suit like the one you wear meant something a lot different."

"Those kings got all the power now though. Why they stay so coaled up?"

"You think that's how things work? Somebody gets power and then chills out? Boy, you slow. How'd it make you feel with that gun in your face? You stay steady? You cool? What if you had the gun and those Pats didn't? What you gonna do?"

John Henry didn't answer. He could still feel the ache of the moment throughout his body. As he finished his walk to Guru's, the moment played over and over in his head. It would keep playing for a while too. His emotions rubber banded from scared to angry to sad. The back and forth drained him. When he walked into Guru's most of it left him, but some of it would stay with him forever he imagined.

"Forget about it, Johnny Steel. Playing it back is what wrecks you. I got some stuff for you to fix. It's on the workbench in the back. Two Ox kits, some headphones and some watches. Once you finish with those, you can look for whatever you want."

"You gonna pay me for those?"

"Of course I'm gonna pay you. What you think a job is? I got some MF Doom and Kendrick Lamar queued up for you. How about you work 'til they finish your lesson."

"Act like I don't know who MF Doom is." John Henry mumbled to himself as he walked to the back.

It wasn't noon yet, so John Henry had time to work and search the bins before heading back for curfew. He heard MF Doom's voice on the speaker doing Monkey Suite as he opened the door to the back. He looked at his SMiRK folded up on the work bench and pictured it as the monkey suit from the song. He wondered if a day would come when he didn't have to wear it everywhere he went.

When the albums finished playing, John Henry had finished fixing all but two of the watches. He stacked the repaired items into two bins he would bring up front to Gibran.

Turning around, he eyed the rows of shelves packed with discarded items and old electronics. John Henry picked one and walked toward it. He didn't dive in but took his time looking up and down. He settled on a shelf and took down one of the bins. It only had cassette players and walkmans, so he left it on the ground. The second bin he took was full of mp3 players. He emptied it to be sure, but it was all the same.

The next bin he pulled down was different than the other two. Instead of being loose electronics, it was packed with small cardboard boxes. The top layer was more mp3 players. He cleared out all of the boxes with the same picture. He pulled out a wide box that had a flat screen computer monitor. The bottom layer made him pause. Underneath the computer monitor box were five smaller boxes each with the picture of an old phone on it. His throat stalled, and he felt his ears get hot. He bit his lower lip as he rubbed his palms together and picked one of the boxes out of the bin.

The phone was heavier than the technology he typically worked on. He turned it over in his hands and pressed the power button, but nothing happened. The phone looked like the right phone, but he didn't know for sure. He would need to pull the phone apart and look at the components.

He gathered the other four boxes and brought all of them to the work bench. He pulled the phones out of their boxes and laid them next to each other. They were identical. Black screens on the front and white covers on the back.

John Henry didn't have the tools for dealing with the phones at Guru's. He would have to take them back home to take them apart. The eshirts he tampered with were at home too and using the phones with the shirts was his main goal. He packed the phones in his backpack and got ready to go. The Pats spooked him, and he wanted to be sure he had time to make it to the subway well before curfew.

John Henry grabbed the bins with the repaired electronics and carried them to the front room.

"I found the phones! Five of them!"

"Are they the right ones?"

"I don't know. I need to take them home to see."

"I never asked. What's your plan with the phones?"

John Henry hesitated. Gibran had gone out on a limb risking giving him a job and a visa without knowing him. It wasn't illegal to do any of that. What John Henry was planning to do with the phones and the eshirts was risky and definitely illegal.

"What? You're not gonna tell me now? How about this, I'll give you the phones for free if you tell me. Otherwise they're going to cost you."

John Henry hadn't thought about paying for five phones. He probably only needed one, but it would be nice if he had spares just in case something broke. He relented.

"I think I can use the phones to control eshirts."

"Okay. I know you know that's illegal. Why you want to mess with that?"

"It's part of my plan to become an emcee. I got the skills, but if I can put on a brash show, I can make it."

"You an emcee? Please smirk, just because you know hip hop doesn't mean you can rap."

The slur did its job to sting and silence John Henry. John Henry thought Gibran might have reservations about him doing something against the Pigeon Code, but he did not expect him to grind him on rapping.

"This is a culture. Blacks have built on it for years to express themselves. Just because your White from Wrashtown doesn't mean you can claim this culture," Gibran followed up.

"Gibran. I know. I've been studying it for years. Just listen to a few lines."

John Henry was about to start rapping when Gibran cut him off.

"Studying? That's exactly what I'm talking about. Get out of here with your dark-skinned ass. Put your SMiRK on and get out of here before curfew comes."

Stunned, John Henry felt the ache from earlier return but this time the tension came with it too. His heart felt tired from beating too hard and his brain felt cooked. He left Guru's without another word.

TRACK 4

JOHN HENRY WAS IN A daze the whole way home. The music in his headphones helped give him the life to get home. Direction. A rhythm to cling to.

It was late, but he got straight to work. He closed himself in his room and put his music on shuffle. The first track to play was "Lost" from Cool Calm Pete. His fingers danced with the tools as he took apart the phones. Soon, only the small internal computers of each device remained on his desk. He used his Ox to scan the parts and get more information. The Ox scan isolated the communication pieces.

The eshirt with the control center taken apart lay nearby. The components looked similar, but he still wasn't sure. He would need to connect both parts to his computer and look at the code.

The intro speech from Public Enemy's "Fight the Power" jarred him from his work. He hadn't heard the song in a while. He tried to work but kept focusing back on the lyrics. The third verse hit him like a ton of bricks. It had been more than a hundred years since Elvis was around, but John Henry had read stories of him capitalizing on Black music.

He remembered Gibran talking about the old Pats. What life was like for them. For Gibran. Living in a community where you might not have much to hold on to. But that's how he felt. He clung to hip hop. It gave him a purpose for living. It gave him something to reach for. Was he stealing

Black music? He didn't think so. He was using it. Building on it. Hip hop pumps life into his veins and he wasn't going to let that die.

He was going to fight the power. He wanted to expel the ache and tension from the Pigeon Police. John Henry settled back into his work more determined than before. He put his head down and started to work on his computer.

A few hours later he stopped working. He had modified a spare watch device with the phone communication components. It looked like a normal watch device just bulkier on the underside. He reassembled the eshirt components.

Now for the moment of truth. He powered up the watch device. He scrolled through a few screens until he found the app tool he created and pressed the button he was looking for. The shirt next on the desk started flashing black and white. It had worked.

John Henry fell back on to his bed and then jumped right back up and turned up the music. He danced around the room to Outkast's "So Fresh, So Clean."

Getting the shirt to work was the first step. John Henry still needed to figure out how he was going to use it. He never envisioned getting this far. He needed time to think.

He decided he was going to head over to Guru's. Even though he barely knew Gibran, he felt he owed it to him to quit in person. He couldn't work there if he felt he was disrespecting Gibran by rapping.

The sun was just beginning to scorch the city. John Henry hadn't slept since he left Guru's. He zombied his way down to the subway station holding on to his backpack straps.

When the subway doors opened, he stepped in and collapsed down into a chair. Each time the car stopped he jolted awake to check the stop. It was an uneasy sleep.

Finally, it was his stop and he headed out on to the street. He wasn't sure if the intermittent sleeping gave him rest or made him more tired. The ache in his body was still there reminding him of yesterday's event. He looked around, grabbed his backpack straps, and walked with purpose to Guru's.

The back door opened for him again. Gibran hadn't revoked his clearance yet. He thought about leaving his SMiRK on because he would be quick, but then decided against it. Face to face was going to be the best.

"Johnny Steel. You already back here? I thought I might not see you again," Gibran said as John Henry walked up to the front.

"I couldn't sleep. I've been thinking all night about what you said."

"You do look tired boy."

"Last night, I was streaming some music while messing with those phones and Public Enemy's 'Fight the Power' came on. The line about Elvis never really meant much to me. Our argument last night broke it loose. Gibran, though, this music is burning up inside of me. All I can think about is rhyming and making beats. With them, I can control my life. Control my pulse. I'm not trying to steal this music. I'm trying to blast this shit to everyone and bring us together."

Gibran squinted at him from his chair behind the counter.

"I know you're not trying to steal hip hop king. I got caught up in the moment yesterday. We were talking about your run in with the Pigeon Pats and it put me in a state of mind. I feel you when you talk about the music beating your heart. I've felt that way a long time.

Not everyone is going to see you and know your passion though. Know your love for this music. You gotta show them. You can't fake this music because it will come out. I've seen when people fake it. You can hear when they fake it. It's not the same. Emceeing isn't just writing rhymes. It's seeing this world around you and connecting it and making it real. Real for you and them. That's when it hits your soul. Takes away your pain."

Gibran's words rang through to his soul. John Henry knew the second thing he was looking for, the perfect collection of rhymes and beats, would take away the ache inside. Make him feel no pain.

Gibran saw the preoccupation in John Henry's eyes and paused before he went on to change the subject.

"What's up with the phones? Were they the right ones?"

Gibran's question shook John Henry from his thoughts.

"They were," John Henry said and hesitated for a moment. "I got it to work."

John Henry pulled out his modified watch device and showed it to Gibran.

"What am I looking at?"

"I integrated the communication pieces of the phone into the computer on the watch. After that I created an app to control my eshirt. Watch."

John Henry pulled the eshirt out of his backpack and messed with his watch. Again, the LED shirt begin to flash.

"That's it?" Gibran asked chuckling. "You gonna use that to kill it on stage?"

John Henry shot him an annoyed look.

"Come on king," he said. "This just proves it works. You need to keep it steady; I'll make it work."

"Before you jump on that, I need you to fix something. It's back on the workbench."

On the bench was a Technics 1200 turntable. John Henry had read about these turntables but never seen one in person. Opening the cover, he gently ran his fingers over it. This was the machine that DJs made their names on.

He plugged it in, hit the power button, and the light turned on. He pressed the start/stop button, but nothing happened. He unplugged it and flipped it over. If it wasn't turning the problem was with the motor. It was direct drive, so the motor was right under the wheel. It allowed DJs to scratch the record with a quick pick up.

John Henry took apart the bottom of the turntable exposing the motor. He looked at it with his Ox. The report told him the rubber on the drive wheel needed replacement. He pushed the part through to the 3d. The 3d spit the part out a few minutes later. He reassembled the turntable and pressed the start/stop button. The wheel on the turntable started spinning.

"Here you go king," John Henry said setting down the turntable on the counter.

"Now cop this," Gibran said as he turned around. He opened a drawer and pulled out a thin square piece of cardboard. From within, he slid out a black vinyl record. "Enter the Wu-Tang on vinyl."

"Steady brash!" John Henry yelled out and he picked up the cardboard cover and looked at the track list. "Wu-Tang is the GOAT. How long you had this?"

"I've had it for a while," Gibran replied. He set the record on the turntable and set the needle to the first cut.

"Bring Da Ruckus" blasted from the speakers behind Gibran.

They let it play through feeling the beat in their bones until RZAs voice brought the final round of the chorus home.

"Damn king, this album always gets me coaled up," John Henry said when it finished.

"Good because I got something else for you." He went on, "I still know a few people from back in the day. While you were fixing the turntable, I called in a favor. I got you set up to perform at the Hive in two weeks."

John Henry stared at him unmoving.

"What?" John Henry didn't get it.

Gibran grabbed John Henry by the shoulders and repeated.

"Johnny Steel, I got you a show at the Hive. In two weeks."

The realization ran through him like electricity until his whole body felt on fire.

"But I haven't figured out what I'm going to do with the eshirts."

"Shit man, you better head out then. You need to put in some work. Can't fuck it up. Make me look bad," Gibran laughed to himself.

John Henry shot him a look.

"I'm just fucking with you. But let me tell you. I got you this show so you can get on stage and do your thing. You got fire. I came around quick, but them heads down there they might not be so welcoming. They might not be quick to look past your SMiRK."

John Henry didn't respond but nodded his head. He was always rapping for himself. He didn't think his skin color would come into the equation. In his imagination, he never pictured a hostile audience.

"Before you go, I got one more track for you," Gibran said as he moved the needle to the last cut on that side of the record.

"Wu-Tang again?" John Henry asked.

"Ah yeah, again and again," Gibran responded and let the record play.

TRACK 5

STILLETTA JAMES' WATCH BLINKED RED and she pulled her arm up to check it. It was a credit deduction notification.

"Fuck!" she muttered to herself and shook her head. "I thought he would wait at least a couple of weeks."

Putting more money into Frank's pocket made her coal hot. She felt it in her face and with the prickling of her skin. It was bad enough he made money on her shows but to owe him personally put salt on the wound.

The credits weren't the problem. She had them. She just rather put them towards herself. With no sponsor, funding her own shows took a lot of upfront money. She needed 500 credits for her next set at The Hive. She would make it all back and then some after the show. Losing the 100 credits put her below what she would need to figure a way to make some more before the show.

Stilletta James feet had been doing the navigating while she thought. She was not paying attention to where she was going. Out of the corner of her eye she saw the police station.

"It was a source of credits," she thought. Not one she liked to take advantage of though. She hadn't since she had been doing shows, but this credit situation put her in a bind.

Stilletta James turned away, walked a few steps, paused, and then turned around and headed back toward the police station.

The bright light and lack of furniture set a severe institutional tone in the reception area. Nobody manned the counter. A receptionist stood to her left but Stilletta preferred dealing with people. She leaned against the counter and craned her neck. No one in sight. With resignation, she went through the routine with the machine.

"Welcome Henrietta," the receptionist said aloud with a slight echo, its friendly tone incongruous with vibe of the room. "How can I help you?"

"I'm here to speak with Officer Gates."

"Commander Gates has been notified you're here. Please wait."

Stilletta stepped back from the receptionist and turned to wait in the corner of the reception area. Unsure of how long she would be waiting, she pulled her headphones on and let her music play. Lupe Fiasco's "American Terrorist" rang through her ears. Her library consisted more of the old school than contemporary.

She stared at the passersby below on the sidewalk. The setting sun negated the colors on the eshirts reducing them to monochrome flashes.

A few songs later, a palm rested on her shoulder. Stilletta James turned to see Commander Gates in a grey uniform.

"Officer Gates," Stilletta said. "How you movin' king?"

"Commander now," he corrected. "I'm doing well. What's got you back here? I don't think I've seen you in the station in a couple of years."

"Still in the grey I see," Stilletta ignored his question, not wanting to seem too eager. "You a Pigeon for life? I thought you would have moved up," she followed up with a little snark.

He led her behind the counter and down the hall.

"Commander ain't no slouch," he countered dropping his proper tone. "I'm running the show now. Not gonna quit until the Graft is done."

"Until the Graft is done," she chuckled. "All the Whites are down with the Graft. You gonna line 'em all up?"

"If that's what it takes." His tone cold and devoid of humor. "The Graft are terrorists. The Whites know who is who. If they don't report them, they're part of the problem."

"Fine by me."

"So, what's up?" he asked as they entered his office. "You didn't come here to give me shit about my career plans. I know you hate the Graft as much as I do, I've heard your songs, but I'm guessing you didn't come here for material."

"Never down to mince. I'm here for work."

"For work? It's been years. What you got for me?"

"That's the thing, king. I don't got anything. I'm looking for work. I need to make some creds."

"What do you need credits for? You're always performing."

"You know how I keep it. Steady straight. No eshirts. No sponsors. Gotta fund my own shows. Shit ain't cheap," she lamented but failed to mention her spending habits. Her lifestyle wasn't cheap.

"You really got nothing," he looked at her sideways. "You're telling me you just happened to come in here and ask me for some work?"

"Yeah king, that's what I'm sayin'."

"Shit this is strange," he said shaking his head. "About a day ago, I got word that Gibran called in a favor for a performance at the Hive."

"Gibran? Shit, I haven't heard his name in a while. I don't think he's performed since before I started."

"He hasn't performed in 10 years. I remember his last show. I was there. The Graft bombed a subway station the day after. 27 people dead, six of them were kids. We swept through Wrashtown and made dozens of arrests. There were riots afterward and a handful of Whites got mirked."

"I remember," Stilletta said almost too quiet to hear. She cast her eyes to the ground and paused.

"I was in middle school," she started again in the same quite tone as if she was in a daze. "My brother was on his way home from his first performance. My parents said I was too young to go. I was so angry with them I locked myself in my room waiting for him to come home. He didn't come home that night. I just figured he was having fun with his friends and was going to come back in the morning. When I woke up my parents were glued to the screen watching the streams on the bombing. They weren't saying anything. My dad had his fork in his hand but the food on the plate hadn't been touched. When Tré's picture flashed on the screen, I broke. I don't know how long I screamed. I can remember my mom cradling me later in my room."

"I'm sorry Stilletta, I didn't know," Gates said as he put his hand on her shoulder. She shied away.

Stilletta sniffled, shook her head, and stood up straight.

"It's okay. It's not your fault. It's their fault, they took him. Why do you think I came to see you when I did?"

"I never thought to ask. I thought you were just patriotic and wanting to make a difference. Looking back that explains a lot."

"Forget about that. What's up with Gibran performing at the Hive? Besides timing, why so strange?"

"He stopped performing after the bombing. Nobody knew why, he just stopped. A few years later he opened Guru's but never performed again. According to my sources he never even talked to his connects at the clubs again."

"I forgot that part of the story. So, he's going to have a show? Lots of people gonna come. He's a legend."

"That's the thing though, he didn't call in a favor for himself to perform. He's putting up someone else to perform."

"What do you mean he put somebody else up to perform? It took me years to get on stage at the Hive."

"The guy he's got lined up is named John Henry. You heard of him?"

"No, never. Where's he from?"

"Word on the street he's a smirk."

Stilletta's face contorted in anger.

"Nah fuck that!" She wanted to spit. Her faced flushed hotter than when she lost her credits earlier. "Can't have no wrash ass smirk rapping on my stage. Malcolm wouldn't put a piece of garbage on stage."

"You better check with Malcom, because I'm telling you this kid is lined up, smirk or not."

Stilletta James exhaled hard.

"I'll check with Malcom."

"Alright, but if you want work, I need more information. I want you to figure out what this kid is doing. Why would Gibran put a smirk on stage out of nowhere? Maybe somebody got something on Gibran and put him up to it. I want you to find out where this John Henry is from and see what ties he has to the Graft. It's been a while since they've claimed something. I don't like how this feels."

"Are you asking me to be friends with this smirk? Shit, fuck that."

"Friends? No. Just figure him out. Plus, I thought you needed credits? It's the night of your show anyway."

This hit her like a punch in the stomach. Her face flashed anger, then went stoic.

"I'll do it, but it's gonna be 200 creds," she stated.

Commander Gates winced and then agreed.

"Okay, but you better come through. I'll get in touch with Malcolm and have him let you do the show on credit. I'll give you 200 credits after you give me something. No information. No credits."

Stilletta hadn't counted on this arrangement. It made sense though. Gates wasn't just going to give her 200 credits for nothing.

"Ok. I'll hit you up." She turned and walked out of his office.

The cold night hit her in the face as she walked out of the police station. The passing eshirts lit up a tear on her cheek. The conversation with Gates unlocked a place in her mind she liked to keep shut. Tré was the one who taught her to rap. Everything she did, she did for him. She figured if she made it big it would be a tribute to him, but she didn't like to think about his death. She didn't like to think about the pictures the media played over and over. These feelings made her sick to her stomach. She wanted to scream into the night, but she wouldn't let herself look weak. She buried Tré deeper inside her mind and tried to forget him.

TRACK 6

STILLETTA JAMES FOUGHT HER WAY through the crowd. She was familiar here and didn't cut the path she did on the street. Some heads turned
and whispered as she walked by. She twisted her body as she pushed
through the crowd making it to a small black door. A man with a device
waited there.

"Yo, Stilletta, what up?" he said as he gave her some daps with one hand
and pulled her in for a hug with the other. "You're on tonight, right?"

"F'sho" she replied. "Got some new songs I'm gonna try out."

He opened the door without looking at the device and let her through.
Behind the door a long hall led further backstage. She walked down the
hall to another door.

The door led to the green room. It had a few couches far enough apart
that you could be alone, but it was small enough that you wouldn't hold a
private conversation. She immediately noticed on the farthest couch was a
person in a SMiRK. She couldn't tell if it was a man or woman by their posture. It had to be John Henry. The Hive didn't exactly have a policy barring
Whites, but none had performed there in her memory.

She recognized most of the other emcees, but the room felt different than normal. The SMiRK clad figure cast a pall over the green room.
Nobody was talking. Nobody was reciting their lyrics to themselves or

moving to a beat. They just glanced at the smirk and then back at each other.

Stilletta James sat at the furthest point from the smirk next to her friend Malcolm, who was also the club manager.

"X, what's with this smirk?"

"I don't know Still. I think I made a mistake. Shit don't feel right."

"Mistake about what?" Stilletta James played it cool trying to get more information from Malcolm.

"Gibran called me up a week ago or so. He said he had a favor to ask. I hadn't talked to him in so long I didn't know how to respond. I thought he might be trying to get back in the game, so I told him anything. He ended up wanting to put this guy up on stage. He said his name was John Henry. I never heard of him, but I said okay. I did a search with my Ox and nothing came up. I didn't know he was a smirk until tonight. The first time I've ever seen one back here. I don't know why he still has it on. They don't need it on."

"That shit makes me uncomfortable. They check him at the door? Would be just like the Graft to send some smirk in here to do some wrash shit."

"They checked him. All he's got is that SMiRK and a few watch devices. I made them check him three times."

"I don't know. Just doesn't feel right."

"I know. I know. I'll watch him. You ready though? You need to get your head right. You're on in a few minutes."

Stilletta James took Malcom's advice and tried to ignore John Henry. His SMiRK conjured images of the Graft and Tré. She closed her eyes but all she could think about was her brother's picture. She tried to bury him in her mind, but he kept coming back. None of these thoughts eased her nerves, but she had to go on. She had to perform a clean set and get legit information from John Henry. Her stream game and credits depended on it.

John Henry felt all the eyes on him as he sat. Gibran had warned him that everyone here would be hostile. John Henry experienced hostility on the street from Blacks before but this carried a different weight. He was back in the green room of the Hive. This was their space. He was the intruder.

When Stilletta James came into the room, his worries about the room disappeared from his mind. John Henry had seen her perform through his Ox, but he never imagined seeing her in person. She was one of his favorites. He liked her style. Her fierce independence. It gave him hope. He figured if he could present a similar image, he could overcome the White stereotype.

She spoke with the club manager for a few minutes. They were both looking his way. He could tell they were talking about him but couldn't make out the words. Disgust played across her face. She turned and walked out.

The room had screens for him to watch the show, but he wanted to see her in person. He got up to follow but then something struck him.

He remembered Gibran's reaction to his SMiRK. The first time he came into Guru's, Gibran made him take it off. His SMiRK repulsed Blacks. He couldn't go out there to watch with his SMiRK on. He planned to take it off for his performance anyway, so he might as well take it off now.

When he came to from these thoughts, he realized everyone had left the room to watch Stilletta James. He worked through the straps and connections on the SMiRK with a mechanical ease and set it in a pile in the corner. Underneath was his modified eshirt. It looked normal. Muted black inside the building.

He walked fast down the hallway to make the beginning of her performance. The hallway led him up to the side of the stage. There was enough room for him to stand and watch the show.

Stilletta James led her performance with the song "Respect My Craft." It was a tribute to the Sun and a scathing rebuke of the Ronald Graft administration. His policies and rhetoric were regarded by the world as the reason the environment was in the condition it was. Blacks loved the song because it ripped the leader who discriminated against them and the terrorists who killed in his name.

John Henry liked the song because he hated wearing the SMiRK. He blamed Graft for their plight. Blamed him for the Flip. Blamed him for the senseless killings of both the Graft and the Pigeon Police.

It was a good anthem to stir up the fire inside. The whole crowd pulsed as one unit as they got into the song. From the side of the stage, he rapped along with the audience on the most prominent lines of the song:

"Mined the oil and coal, gotta make that money
But the jokes on you cuz my outlook is sunny.
We went toe to toe Mr. President Graft
Now I'm burning a hole you best respect my craft."

She commanded the stage and the crowd. Each rhyme flowed from her with authority. John Henry watched her in rapt attention. His body moved to the beat on its own. Stilletta James finished the song and the crowd erupted.

She continued through her set. Each song pulling the crowd in and taking them on a lyrical ride. Sweat beaded on her forehead but she looked energized instead of tired.

"This last song I want to dedicate to my brother Tré. The Graft killed him when he was young. Just getting started. He inspired me to be who I am," Stilletta James said and then held up the microphone with one hand and bowed her head down. She stayed in this position until the beat dropped. A slower, more pensive song than the others.

John Henry had never heard the song before. He sympathized with her because he never knew his dad. The Pigeon Police killed his dad when he was little.

Before he could think about it too much, he felt a tap on his shoulder. It was the club manager, Malcom.

"You the smirk?" Malcolm ask him.

John Henry bristled at the slur but nodded.

"I though you would be whiter," he said and went on without waiting for a response. "Maybe it will help you out on stage. I'm not trying to have a riot in here. You're up next though."

The reminder of his Whiteness and the notice he was on next put him off balance. John Henry started to sweat, and his stomach tightened.

John Henry came back to reality as Stilletta James was coming off stage.

"That was brash," he told her. He forgot her last song was about her brother and realized he might have sounded insensitive. "Sorry about your brother," he added.

"Thanks," she said. She looked at him trying to place his face but couldn't.

They continued looking at each other for a second. Neither one knowing what to say next.

"Here I go," John Henry said to break the silence and headed on stage.

The realization he was the smirk washed over her. A bitter taste developed in her mouth as she felt her disgust come rushing in.

"So not what you were expecting either?" Malcom asked with a bit of fun his voice, knowing it would irritate her.

"Get the fuck out of here," she responded with a similar tone. "I forget that every smirk isn't white skinned underneath those sheets."

They both watched John Henry as he prepared. It didn't look like he was doing much. He just kept messing with his watches.

"This will be interesting," Stilletta James told Malcolm. Her disgust faded a little as her curiosity about his performance increased.

John Henry walked up to the center of the stage and grabbed the microphone. The crowd gave a murmur in anticipation.

He was too nervous to talk to the crowd. Even if he wasn't, he wouldn't know what to say. He knew his songs backwards and forwards. He recited them everywhere he went, but he had never thought about actually being here. He never thought he would really ever perform his songs.

He was thinking about his eshirt. It worked with his songs at his apartment, but this is where his confidence faltered. Would all the shirts link like he planned? He wouldn't know until he tried.

Somebody close to the stage yelled something about starting and he focused.

He looked down at his watch device and started his song through his app. The speakers behind and around him responded with the beat to his first song.

This was it. This was the moment. His shirt was supposed to light up when the next layer of beats came in.

Stilletta watched John Henry from the side of the stage. She didn't want to be there. Her last song about her brother had drained her and stoked smoldering feelings of resentment at the Graft. Watching a smirk perform right after her isn't how she pictured the song being delivered. It stung.

She wanted to leave. To walk into the fresh air of the night and enjoy the catharsis of being alone. Untouchable.

But she had told Gates she would look into John Henry. See what the Graft was up to. She had to do it for him for the credits, but she felt like she owed it to Tré.

She watched him hit his watch and felt the beat come in. It was better than she expected but maybe it was because she didn't expect much from the smirk.

Then his shirt flashed. But not just his. Everyone in the audience's eshirts did too. The light was dazzling and blinded her. For a second, she thought there was some sort of state mandated emergency reporting going on. By the movement of the crowd, she could tell she wasn't the only one who was confused.

These thoughts dropped from her mind as she realized the flashing was synchronized with John Henry's beats. The crowd realized a few seconds later and stopped moving.

She was never interested in the eshirts. She hated what the stood for and how they trapped people into debt with lures and promises. But now she couldn't take her eyes off of the light show playing before her eyes. The beats and colors were mesmerizing.

He finished his first song. The beats and the lights went quiet. So did the audience. Or rather the audience remained quiet. They were still trying to figure out what had happened. Too confused to applaud or get into the show. Stilletta hadn't paid attention to any of his lyrics. She was too transfixed by the lights.

The lights started up again and John Henry went into his next song.

"We thrash in the wrash, hit the bottom of rock.
Like termites in the sun, when the Pigeon Pats squawk."

These lyrics grabbed her attention. With the initial shock of the eshirts behind her, Stilletta James could focus more of her attention on John Henry.

He rapped on.

"Ya'll praising the Flip, but it feels like a flop.
Now we underground, when ya'll shining on top."

John Henry was focused on his lyrics. Trying to block out everything and rap on stage. He didn't have his eyes open engaging the audience. Stilletta James did though and she could feel the audience turning. Coming to the realization that the rapper on stage was different.

A few versus later they realized the difference.

"We're dragging our feet, leaning ready to fall,
Hundreds of bunions, some small and some Paul.
Losing our shoulders, our posture, our fight,
Looking for Blacks, to help the plight of the White.
We burnin' and dyin', not all of us Graft.
Gone with the wind, while ya'll have the last laugh."

John Henry didn't see the first object thrown at him from the crowd, but he felt the second. It was bottle and it glanced off his arm. His whole head followed it as he watched it land behind him and shatter. As he turned forward, several more bottles hit him in the body. A metal cup hit him in the face dropping him to the ground.

Stilletta James watched from the side. Everything happening in slow motion for her. As she listened to John Henry's lyrics, she felt the crowd's anger rise with hers, but she didn't expect the thrown bottle.

Now she was looking at John Henry lying on the stage. Unsure if he was unconscious. The only thing she could think of in that moment was that his faced looked just like the pictures of her brother that were played over and over again on the news after the bombing. Before she knew and it before anyone could rush the stage, she found herself dragging John Henry off stage by his shirt. By the time she got to the edge of the stage, he was coming to.

She helped him up and shoved him through an exit to the street.

"We gotta get you out of here."

She pushed him down the sidewalk. John Henry was standing up and walking but his ears were still ringing from what just happened.

Stilletta James couldn't figure out why she was still helping him, only she couldn't stop thinking of her brother.

A sharp cold wind bit into their faces.

"My SMiRK!" John Henry exclaimed as he looked up to the sky. A full moon shown bright.

"It's back at the Hive. You can't go back. Not with what you just kicked up in there. They fuckin' coaled up. It looked like an anti-Graft rally in there. They'll probably mirk you if they catch you. You tryin' to die? What the fuck were you thinking with those lyrics?"

John Henry ignored the question.

"I gotta get to the subway," John Henry said with anxiety. He saw the closest tunnel a block up and started to run.

She kept following him. Not moving with the same urgency. She got to the top of the tunnel and squinted down.

"How did you sync the shirts with your beats?" Stilletta James yelled down the stairs. She realized her curiosity was the other reason she was helping him.

No response. She hated going into the subway. She took a few steps down.

John Henry was a lot closer than she expected in a shadow just under the tunnel. She paused. He was thinking.

"If you really want to know, meet me at Guru's on Wednesday. I'll show you." Then he turned and vanished around a corner into the depths of the subway station.

Her feelings of disgust and curiosity swirling together making her head light. She looked up at the moon and headed back on to the street.

TRACK 7

JOHN HENRY TUGGED AT THE straps of his SMiRK and stretched his arms out. The spare he found in the closet was from high school. He had grown since then. The SMiRK was a loose garment for the most part, so he just needed to make the proper adjustments to get it right. He would be messing with it for the rest of the day.

John Henry walked toward Graft park, still adjusting his gloves.

He needed time to think and the park was his refuge. It was where he went when he wanted to write or take time to think through a difficult repair problem.

He surveyed that park as he walked toward the statue of Graft on the other end. As usual, there was no one around.

In the 20s, President Ronald Graft had commissioned thousands of parks across the country. At the time, he said they were for jobs, but it was really for his ego. These parks in most communities were in disrepair now. Whites blamed Graft for the Flip, so they stayed out of them. Blacks hated Graft for his racist and violent policies, so they stayed out of them. The parks weren't maintained by anyone.

This made it the perfect place to think. No one was ever in the park to distract John Henry.

He looked at the statue of President Graft as he sat down. Someone had tried to pull it down years ago but failed so the Graft stood there leaning forward. Perpetually looking like he was about to fall on his face.

John Henry came here to think about the night before. He had been replaying it in his head over and over. He remembered turning his head and getting hit in the face hard. The next thing he knew Stilletta James was dragging him off stage. Before he split with her at the subway, she had told him the crowd could have mirked him in the frenzy.

He thought about his lyrics. The song was meant as a call for help. He wanted the crowd, Blacks, to see things from a different angle. Maybe spark a conversation. Instead they rained projectiles on him. That's not how he pictured his first show going. In his head he always left to a standing ovation. An angry mob was a far throw from that.

The eshirts had worked though! He chuckled out loud to himself and shook his head. They worked better than he could have imagined. He had a lot to learn about performing, but controlling the shirts had everyone in there in awe and wonder.

He repeated the lyrics to his first song out loud.

"I blast LED tees,
Make your heart freeze,
Cold as ice, like the dice,
When you losing ten g's."

"That's quite the verse," a voice said from behind him.

John Henry jumped up and spun around. A man in a shiny green SMiRK stood leaning against the base of the Graft statue.

"Thanks," John Henry mumbled, a little embarrassed. "I thought I was alone. There's usually no one here."

He had read about green SMiRKs and seen them in pictures but never in person. Only the Graft wore them. John Henry looked around to see if anyone else was around. The Graft were terrorists. They bombed innocent people including other Whites. They were wanted by the Pigeon Police. The more John Henry thought about it, the more nervous he became.

"I don't think I should be here," John Henry blurted out into the silence that was lingering between the two. "With you," he added.

"Why not?" the man replied chuckling. "You said it yourself no one is ever here."

The man's laughter made John Henry even more uneasy.

"I could get in trouble. People might think I'm Graft. Almost was mirked last night. I don't need any more trouble," John Henry rattled off, trying to think of a way to get out of the situation. He didn't want to just run off. He didn't know if he was in danger or not and he didn't want to spark anything. He already misjudged one dangerous situation and didn't want to do it again.

"We're not all bad," the man said. "In fact, we're not bad at all. Just trying to look out for each other. Plus, I wanted to come say hi great gramps." As he said this, he patted the foot of the Graft statue.

The man continued to unsettle John Henry. His voice although calm and quiet, felt dangerous and crazy. How could he say they were looking out for Whites, when they killed them in bombings? John Henry kept the question to himself. He didn't want to trigger this man.

"Great gramps?" John Henry asked in attempt to keep the conversation light.

"Yeah, President Graft. That's great grandpa. He was a son of a bitch. I'm Ronald Graft the fourth," he said and stepped forward and held out his hand.

John Henry's heart jumped in his chest and started sprinting. This wasn't just a member of the Graft. Ronald Graft IV was *the* Graft. He was their self-proclaimed supreme leader.

John Henry looked around and again to see if anyone was around or watching. Now he really wanted to get out of here. He grabbed his hand to shake it not wanting to anger Ronald Graft IV.

"It's a funny thing about people," Ronald Graft IV continued on. "They say they know the Graft. That we're terrorists, killing innocent people. But do we really?"

"I've seen you claim attacks on streams," John Henry blurted out in reply, forgetting his concerns for a second.

"You know streams. You've seen AR plenty of times. How do you really know? Why would we kill Whites when we're trying to save them?"

John Henry thought to himself. He had seen altered reality video many times. It was hard to know anything from a stream was not doctored or even completely made up.

"If that's the case, why don't you ever come out against it?" John Henry asked still feeling suspicious, but the life and death fear was starting to subside.

"If we did that, do you think you would believe it?" asked Robert Graft IV.

"Probably not," John Henry conceded.

"There you go. If you, a SMiRK living in Wrashtown in the heart of oppression, wouldn't change your mind, then who would? It wouldn't be worth my time. No, we just keep pushing in the shadows. Trying to bring back honor to the founding fathers and restore Whites to where they should be."

As he talked his voice grew colder and John Henry could detect a hint of anger, reminding him of the of danger of the situation.

"On equal footing with Blacks," Robert Graft IV said in a sarcastic tone making it hard to know if he was being serious or if it was just for show.

John Henry didn't trust him at all. He gave him the creeps. It was a good thing they couldn't see each other's faces because John Henry would have given himself away.

"Which is where you come in."

This sentence made the hair on John Henry's neck bristle.

"I wanted to talk to you about the little trick you pulled with the eshirts last night at the Hive."

"How do you know about that?" John Henry asked.

"It's all over the streams. Don't you know?"

He didn't. He was lost in his own thoughts and hadn't even thought to check the streams this morning. He didn't think it would have been a big deal.

From the silence, Robert Graft IV gathered he didn't know.

"The general narrative is that you were Graft intentionally there to start a riot."

This got John Henry coaled up.

"That's bullshit. Anyone watching a repeat of the show could tell I was caught off guard."

"Really? You think so," Robert Graft IV asked. "Look at this."

Robert Graft IV held out his watch. John Henry was reluctant, but he held his watch out next to Graft's and linked his Ox. The video began to play. It was surprisingly grainy and from a weird angle. Not the typical stream the Hive puts out for shows. It showed his performance. You couldn't really see his facial reactions on stage. It looked like he did his performance, waited for the crowd to get angry, and then turned and crawled offstage. It was hard to make out Stilletta James helping him off.

Was that how it looked? He thought to himself. That's not how he remembered it.

"See what I mean about AR?" Robert Graft IV broke John Henry's attention to the stream.

"I guess. I mean, I see what you mean," John Henry mumbled in shock. "So, people think I'm Graft now…"

He thought back to the police encounter he had a few weeks earlier. If he was associated with the Graft, they would have arrested him on the spot maybe even killed him regardless of visa.

"That's not such a bad thing," Robert Graft IV comforted him. "Maybe we can help each other out. Maybe this was meant to be."

"How's that?"

"If you share your little eshirt trick with the Graft, I can issue a stream stating you weren't linked to us."

This didn't make any sense to John Henry. If he gave them the technology and they used it, even if the Graft came out and distanced themselves from John Henry, as soon as they used the technology people would assume he was Graft and go right back to square one.

He didn't want to come right out and deny Robert Graft IV in this isolated scenario.

"What would you use it for?" John Henry asked trying to stall to think of a way out.

"Come on now. Use your brain SMiRK. We could unite the Whites and disrupt the Blacks and Pigeons. Give us a leg up in the fight. Take back what's ours. Think about not having to wear a SMiRK again? What would that look like? An equal world."

John Henry didn't think this was reality. He had heard the extreme preaching of the Graft before. They had all kinds of crazy theories to revert the atmosphere and fix the sun problem, setting off nuclear bombs, building a cover around the Earth, the list went on. They were all equally farfetched and psycho. Most of them would likely kill the planet or everyone on it.

On a personal level, John Henry had worked for years trying to figure out the eshirt technology. He felt like it was his. Even if the Graft could somehow get him out of a SMiRK, he didn't want to just give it up to a guy he just met.

"I can't give it to you," John Henry finally said.

"Why not?" Robert Graft IV asked.

"It's mine. It took me a long damn time to figure it out and I'm the only one who can do it. I'm not just going to give it to you." John Henry said, finding some courage deep down.

"You're going to turn your back on your own people because of your pride?"

"That's not how I see it king," John Henry said, knowing it would coal Robert Graft IV up.

"Don't fucking call me that! You're making a big mistake Johnny boy."

"Maybe I am. Salaam," he said, and he started walking off.

"Hey John, I'll see you around," Robert Graft IV called out after he was an arms throw away. "Power to the Fathers."

Robert Graft finished the salute by putting his hand over his heart.

The gesture and tone of his voice made John Henry's blood run cold.

TRACK 8

STILLETTA JAMES HADN'T LEFT HER apartment for a couple of days. After she had left John Henry at the subway station, she had gone straight home. All she could remember was picturing John Henry as her brother and then running out to drag him off the stage before he could be over-taken. It was like a dream. She didn't remember moving her own body. It was like she was watching a stream of the show from backstage.

She couldn't bring herself to check the real streams until the next morn-ing. She was worried people would see the footage of her with John Henry and think she was a friend of his. Think that maybe she was a part of the whole thing. Being associated with him or even having people know she saved him could ruin her image. She had fought hard to be where she was, and she still had a long way to go. If the crowd thought she was a friend of the Whites, her verses would be laughable.

"Respect my craft?" she said out loud to herself. "Lookin' more like a fan of the Graft..."

"Fuck!" she shouted putting both hands behind her head. She let them fall as she sighed and lowered her head.

"Show me streams," she said. Finally, willing to face them.

She watched the video. The grainy quality surprised her. The metal cup flew and hit John Henry. He went down and then he was moving off stage.

You could kind of see a shadow hovering over him in the video, but it didn't really look like anything. She only knew it was her because she was there.

She was relieved and annoyed at the same time. Someone had spent time to put some AR into it to take her out of it.

Why would they do that? She thought to herself. Was it the Pigeon Police trying to twist it? The AR version definitely made it look like John Henry knew what he was doing. He didn't, she thought. And someone had taken time to diminish her presence in the video. She became less annoyed as the curiosity overtook her.

The streams accused John Henry of being a Graft agitator. Several of the heads claimed this blatant disregard for the eshirt rules and the Pigeon Code was a test for something bigger from the Graft.

"It didn't seem like it." She remembered how young John Henry looked. She kept thinking of her brother even though they didn't look alike. How was John Henry so black? Did he really need the SMiRK?

Since now she knew the Pigeon Police weren't after her for helping John Henry, she thought she would meet up with Gates to see if she could find out more. Unless the Pigeon Police had doctored it to make it a bigger deal than it was? Maybe Gates had her erased to protect her? She had heard of Whites accusing the Pigeon Police of doctoring streams, but always thought they were made up. Had they been using AR with Whites all of this time? The questions kept coming.

The last few thoughts made her a little nervous about talking with Gates, but he was the only way to figure out what was going on. Plus, maybe she could find out more about John Henry if she went to talk to him. Was he just a naïve SMiRK trying to rap or was he something else?

The afternoon Sun shone through the windows of the police station as Stilletta James walked into the lobby. She looked at the receptionist box and said, "Commander Gates." The receptionist went through the scan routine and then produced a screen "5 minutes wait."

The Graft hysteria had risen from the normal humdrum bogeyman references the streams used to make to front and center. Heads were trying to guess the next move. They reminded viewers the Graft hadn't bombed in three years. Pigeon Police representatives went on to tout their successes and calm the public. She had even seen Gates in one. It only fed into it.

"Please proceed to Commander Gates' office," the receptionist sounded through Stilletta's headphones momentarily stopping her music. The door to the inside of the police station slid open with a hiss.

She tapped her watch once to turn off her music and headed down the hall. Coming towards her were four men, the one in the front had on a shiny gold choker necklace.

"Miss little pretty Nubian, what you doin' here," he said. The four of them filling the hallway forcing her to respond in some fashion.

"I thought there was only men back here. Got yourself bitched out like a pit with that collar," Stilletta James rose up to his face.

"Hah," he laughed in her face. "All coaled up. So sensitive Stilletta. Don't be so green queen."

Her nose flared at the thought of her being jealous of him. She hated that he was making her mad. She relaxed and smiled.

"Doomsday and the horsemen, of course then," she chuckled. "Ya'll just some asses, rubbin' elbows with some ashes, like flour clashes, couldn't make a mouthful for Samson when he slay the masses."

The rhyme flowed off her tongue without hesitation.

"Stilletta James, I know your game. Break through the windowpane, you know I win this game," he tried back.

"Good game, Doomgame," Stilletta laughed and pushed her way through the horsemen.

As she walked down the hall, he shouted after her.

"You can't see these creds though!"

"You brash! prince," she shouted back without turning. Her smile transitioned to a scowl. "How the fuck does that dude make so much money. Rhyming game and game? What a fuckboy," she thought to herself.

She entered Commander Gates' office. He was staring blankly. Stilletta James could tell he was engaged in his Ox, so she stood there to wait. He clicked his watch a couple of times and then swiped a few times in the air. He hit is watch once more and then turned to look at Stilletta James.

She spoke first.

"You workin' with zombies now?"

"Who called you a zombie?" he responded.

"Shit, I'm not talking 'bout me. I'm talking 'bout Doomsday and his horseboys."

"Hey, I need to get information. They told me they were at the Hive that night. Plus, you haven't showed up until now. Where have you been? The Graft pulling more shit than they've done in years and you're waiting to come in."

This statement threw Stilletta James off. She figured Gates had doctored the video to keep her out of trouble. His reaction made it seem like he didn't know her part in it. Or was he playing it off? But if he didn't mess with it, then who? With all the questions still swirling in her mind she decided to play it as cool as possible and not give away anything.

"You know how I work," she said. "I didn't want to come flyin' in here blastin' everything the next morning. That would give away my leverage. I need to get more information from John Henry. I can't have him thinking I'm talking to the Pigeon Police. Then he'll freeze me out for sure."

"So, you talked to him then?" Gates asked.

"Yes and no. I saw him in the green room in his SMiRK and then he changed to go on stage, while I was performing. He went on after me, but I didn't realize until he was up on stage. His skin was as black as yours and mine are, so I didn't know it was him until the eshirts started flashing and he was rhyming about saving the Whites. Then it was all a blur. I tried to catch up with him as he was running out...."

Stilletta James didn't know if she wanted to give away she had talked with him and was planning on meeting him up.

"And?" Gates asked.

Stilletta James continued to think about the night and what had happened. She played the stream of her pulling him off the stage again in her head.

"Stilletta," Gates broke her concentration. "John Henry is likely Graft. This looks like a test for something bigger. Who knows what they'll try and pull next time? Maybe they use it to trigger another bomb like the one that killed your brother. What then Stilletta?"

She looked down. Normally, she would be fuming with anger. She used to feed this hatred to get coaled up and do shows. Now, she just felt empty inside. She pictured her brother and then thought of John Henry.

"I don't think he's Graft," she said in a soft voice. "He just seemed harmless."

She thought back to picturing him rapping with his eyes closed on stage. She remembered doing that her first times on stage because of nerves.

"I think he just wanted to rap, and it got out of hand."

"That's what you think?" Gates asked.

He tapped his watch a couple of times, slid his hands in the air, and then the screen on the wall lit up. It took Stilletta James a few moments to focus in on what it was. The picture was a scene of a park but zoomed pretty far out. She narrowed in on the only two figures in the park. A white SMiRK and a green SMiRK. She had never seen a green SMiRK before.

"The meta in this stream identifies the white SMiRK as John Henry. You ever see a green SMiRK before?" Gates asked.

"No, I don't think so."

"You don't see them because they don't show themselves very often. A green SMiRK is Graft royalty. I mean *the* Graft royalty. The meta says that's Ronald Graft IV. So, your guy here, the day after the Hive, is sitting in the park talking with the Graft. I'm talking *the* Graft and you expect me to believe he's not working with the Graft?"

"Where did you get these photos? Why didn't you just go get them then?"

"We don't monitor the Wrashtown footage as much as the Pigeon Line sector let alone Graft park. No one is usually there. Anyways it trickled in this morning when the meta filters finally got to it."

Gates scrolled through several more pictures on the screen. Even though they were in SMiRKs, it was clear they were talking. The last photo showed them parting ways, the green SMiRK giving the Graft salute. Stilletta James could almost hear the "Power to the Fathers" in her head.

Her mind was racing. Could John Henry really be Graft? Did she pull him off stage and prevent an attack? Was she in danger if she met up with him? No, he was almost unconscious when she started dragging him. A cold-blooded terrorist would not be dragged off the stage and then decide to meet up. It didn't make any sense. But what about the pictures? She thought to the AR and couldn't know if anything was real at this point.

"I was able to talk to him after the show," she said.

"Why didn't you say that earlier?" Gates demanded.

"You were on your Graft rant."

Gates rolled his eyes.

"Ok then, what did he say."

"I'm meeting him up in a couple of days at Guru's. I can get a better take then. I'll be able to tell you if he's Graft or not."

She didn't know if that were true, but she wanted more time for herself. Time to ask John Henry about the eshirts and how he did it. She wasn't lying though because she was going to ask him about the Graft pictures too.

"Where are you meeting him?"

"He asked me to meet him at Guru's. I thought that was a safe place."

"Okay, I'll let you do this, but I'm holding the credits until we talk again. I can't have you running off and not getting to the bottom of this. I can't have a terrorist attack on my hands. I don't think you want that either."

Stilletta James walked out. A million thoughts running through her head. Was she sure he wasn't Graft? Was her life in danger? Who the fuck did Doomsday think he was? Even her inner monologue wasn't over the encounter.

TRACK 9

IT WAS WEDNESDAY. THE DAY John Henry had told Stilletta James to meet him at Guru's. John Henry was nervous to make the trip over to Guru's. He had watched the stream of the show at the Hive several times. The footage, with spin from the heads, had his name on all of the streams. If he was worried about the Pigeon Police before, it was going to be even worse when they were looking for him.

John Henry couldn't forget his conversation with Robert Graft IV either. Why did he want his eshirt technology? What was his plan? That guy made him nervous. He felt like a ticking time bomb. When he went off, John Henry didn't want to be in his blast radius.

He felt like he was inserted into a chess game between the Pigeon Police and the Graft. The longer he was in the game the more likely he was going to be collateral damage. Was it the Graft or the Pigeons who doctored the video? He felt like each one could have done it for their own gain.

The more John Henry thought about the situation the less he wanted to head over to Guru's. It was a big risk. If the Pigeon Police picked him up, he would go to jail for sure. Even if he hadn't done anything. With all the hysteria in the streams, it would be hard for them not to charge him with something. But the more he thought about it the more reasons were spurring him to leave.

He needed more phones. The last time he was at Guru's he was too excited to perform and had left all of the other phones there. If he was going to use his technology to get him out of this, he needed all of the help he could get. The more phones gave him a better chance of negotiating with the Pigeon Police and the Graft.

He really wanted to meet with Stilletta James. He loved her rhymes, her persona. John Henry thought if there were a chance to perform again, it would be through her. If he stood her up, he's not sure if he would ever meet with her again.

Finally, someone was going to come looking for him. Pigeon Pats or Graft. If he was home when they came, it could get his mom involved too. He wanted to keep her out of it as much as possible. If he was on the move, maybe he could figure things out until the streams chilled out. He had enough creds after the show that would get him by for a couple of days.

John Henry put his backpack on. He picked up a few watch devices. He had formatted a few and downloaded fake data on to them. A chipped watch would get him through subway stations and check points with no questions. If something had to scan his eye that was a different story. He didn't have an answer for that. He would just have to avoid the Pigeon Pats and couldn't engage any robots.

Before he left, he had one thing he wanted to check. What if the Pigeon Pats had been to Guru's to talk to Gibran before he got there? If Gibran told them everything, they could confiscate the phones or worse be there waiting to arrest him.

John Henry powered on the phone device he used to control the eshirts. These old devices took a minute or two to boot up. He flipped through some icons on the screen until he found the app he was looking for. Clicking on the link took him to a map screen showing five phone icons clustered together. They were all hovering over the block where Guru's was.

"Good," John Henry said to himself. "At least I know they are all in the same place. Hopefully there is no surprise waiting for me there."

He thought about messaging Gibran, but if there really was a trap what good would that do? The Pigeon Pats would just intercept and tell him to come anyway. At this point, it was a risk he had to take.

The streams were blasting his video and his face the entire ride on the subway. He remembered this sort of coverage on past Graft attacks, but he never thought he would be on the receiving end of it especially since he hadn't even done anything. They had attacked him. He was starting to get angry at the AR video for the story it told. It made him think back to all of the videos he had seen from the Pigeon Pats showing altercations and mirkings. His blood was getting hot.

This was the first time in his life where he felt thankful for the SMiRK. Nobody could tell who he was. He didn't have to worry about someone shouting to the police. On the other hand, no one could see how angry he was. His face was hot and flush. The scowl he had on under his hood wouldn't have done him any favors for avoiding attention.

The lyrics in his headphones brought his mind in focus but did little to ease his anger. The voice of Biggie Smalls rapping about pulling burners flooded into his ears. The lines slowed his pulse but sharpened his coal. He felt it was him against the world. The Pigeon Pats and streams calling him a terrorist and the Graft trying to get him to do their dirty work.

John Henry walked out of the subway station in this mood. The first time he was not thinking about the Pigeon Police. Not because he wasn't worried, but because he was so focused. His mind focusing on every lyric pumping through his headphones and his pulse in line with the rhythm.

A block past the subway station the track ended. The silence brought the anxiety the beats had held at bay. His recent travels past the Pigeon Line had made him aware of the limited peripheral vision the SMiRK afforded the wearer. He found himself turning all the way around just to see what was behind him because a mere glance wouldn't do the job. It felt ridiculous but it was the only way to quell his anxiety.

The moment the music stopped his skin prickled and he felt the urge to turnaround. He did it and kept walking backwards to keep him on his path. Nobody behind him. He was worrying for nothing. The next track started up and he turned back around.

When he turned back the way he was going. There were four figures walking toward him. Were they there the entire time and he didn't notice because of the music? No, he was sure he would have noticed.

John Henry didn't know what to do. He felt if he turned to run, they would chase him. Even if he managed to outrun them, he would have to wait at the subway station, and they would catch him there. Running would show weakness. But if he kept on going, there were four of them and only one of him. He didn't see a scenario where he would win any sort of fight. Maybe they would walk right past him and he was worried about nothing.

Then he saw their faces and knew this wasn't the case. They were from the front row of his set. He wouldn't have remembered from the night alone, but he had seen the footage enough by now that he recognized all of their faces.

"How you rollin' smirk?" the lead one asked. John Henry was pretty sure he was Doomsday. The lead rapper in a group called the Four Horsemen. The numbers matched up.

"Steady king," John Henry tried to say with a tone of nonchalance. Maybe if he played it cool, nothing would happen.

"Steady king…." Doomsday repeated John Henry's words. "That's funny because you didn't look steady last time we met. Caught you duckin' out like a bitch."

John Henry knew what Doomsday was trying to do. Even with AR and all, Doomsday didn't want to have to deal with explaining mirking a White without cause, but if he could get John Henry to do something first. It was fair game. He wouldn't get in trouble at all. Might even get some positive stream from it and maybe a bump in his deals. That's how this type of thing worked.

John Henry knew he was in a dangerous situation. He decided to keep walking. They all turned and walked with him. Doomsday kept right in his face. The SMiRK shielded his fear and sweat from the Horsemen.

"So, which is it SMiRK, you steady or you a bitch?"

"Steady king," John Henry mumbled out.

"What was that? Sounded like bitch to me. You lucky we didn't get you last time. Would have mirked your ass that night," Doomsday laughed in his face and all of the others laughed around him.

John Henry face continued to heat up. The lyrics he just listened to shot through his mind and broke his anxiety and upped his confidence.

"It's more than a few feet from the wrash smirk. You lose your Ox?" Doomsday went on.

"Nah, I'm steady king. Just tryin' to get to work."

"You catch that Fam? This smirk trying to get to work. I didn't know they were letting smirks suck dick this side of the Pigeon Line."

John Henry knew it wasn't a good idea, but he couldn't hold back any longer. He was already in trouble on some level so he might as well embrace the situation.

"My bad king, I didn't know this was your dick sucking spot. Didn't know I was up against the champ." John Henry said knowing he was playing with fire.

"Aww shit Doom, smirk coming at ya," the horseman named Famine said with a chuckle in his voice.

Doomsday's body language went from playful and slack to rock hard. His face twisted in anger.

"Fuck you smirk, you don't know me," Doomsday snapped back and spit on John Henry's SMiRK.

John Henry grinned under his smirk just a little bit. He had struck a chord.

"That's what I'm saying king. I don't know you. I didn't know this was your show. I'll pack up my dick sucking and be on my way. You can have all the dicks."

Doomsday grabbed John Henry's SMiRK and brought up him close to his face. The goggles were dark so Doomsday couldn't see his eyes.

"Don't fuck with me smirk! We'll fucking mirk you right here!" Doomsday yelled in his face.

Doomsday let him go. It seemed he remembered his plan of inciting John Henry and not getting himself into trouble. John Henry felt the transition. He thought he might be getting the upper hand.

"Why were you watching my show anyways? Taking notes? How to rhyme better?" John Henry kept going.

He could see Doomsday wanted to hit him but wasn't doing anything. The five of them were just walking down the street.

"You gon let him do you like that Doom?" Conquistador piped in. Famine and Warlord were eyeing the both of them. Seeing how everything was going to play out.

"Shut the fuck up Conk! I told you I would handle this," Doomsday chirped back. "I don't need your wrash ass rhymes. Get the fuck out of here!" He kept clenching and unclenching his fists but didn't do anything.

John Henry had an idea. He was only two blocks out from Guru's. If he could distract them the rest of the way, maybe he could slip into Guru's. These guys wouldn't try anything in Guru's.

John Henry nodded his head to an internal beat, withdrew into his mind, and then proceeded to bust.

"Wrash ass rhyme time? You wanna go primetime?
I heard the chime, for whom did the bell dime?
Yo time is nigh, so best not even try
Look at the sky, and got you askin' God why?"

Fucking bummer, you're seeing ya blunder.
"Who the fuck am I?", I got you to wonder
A sick fuck, a dick suck, homophobic quick buck.
Nip tuck ya face chub, doom the day God made ya."

"Aww shit Doom, he droppin' bars." Conquistador blurted out again. He seemed to enjoy riling up Doomsday. "Get'em Doom. Show him some coal!"

John Henry kept walking hoping to make it to Guru's.

Doomsday was pacing back and forth quick enough to keep up. John Henry couldn't tell what he was going to do. He half felt like he was about to bust but maybe Doomsday was going to jump him instead.

"I'm motherfucking Doomsday, reppin' this collar
When I'm in play, get your girl to holla.
You want this coal, then I'm sending you fire
Smoking you out, like I'm burning these tires.

You walkin' alone besta watch your back
I got your rope and I'm cutting no slack.
You just a bitch, weak rhymes, and a smirk.
Watch your head because we fixin' to mirk."

Doomsday's last line sunk into John Henry's mind. The sobering reality hit him in the gut. It didn't matter if he was a better rhymer or a quicker wit. They were planning on killing him.

"Speechless smirk?" Famine clapped at John Henry.

He had to play it cool, but his heart was beating out of his chest. The menace of the situation continued to tighten in his chest.

He remembered one block to Guru's.

"Just don't know how to respond to some weak ass rhymes fam," John Henry said in a subdued tone.

"What was that? You still talking shit mothafucka. You gotta death wish smirk," Doomsday snarled right in his face.

"Not a death wish, just wish you could rhyme better. I was hoping for some competition."

As they were approaching the last block, John Henry's heart sunk in his chest. The Pigeon Police who had hassled him a couple of weeks ago were walking toward the five of them. He wasn't making it to Guru's. He turned around real quick deciding to run, but Warlord was right behind him.

"Where you going smirk?" he said and pushed him back the way he was going.

"Now what's up, mothafucka," Doomsday said as he pushed him too.

John Henry thought he would try one last thing.

"Officers! I'm just trying to get back to the Wrash. Back to my side. These guys are keeping me here. I'm just trying to follow the rules. Can you take me back to the Wrash?" John Henry pleaded. His voice cracked and his fear showed at last.

Both of their faces were stoic. It was as if they didn't even here him. His vision started to narrow and get dark from the sides. His breathing quickened and his body prickled with heat.

"Is this man bothering you?" the younger officer asked. John Henry looked up with a glimmer of hope that the pigeon pat actually heard him, but the officer was looking at Doomsday and pointing at him.

"Yeah, king. He's been following us trying to start a fight. We've been trying to ignore him."

"That's a fucking lie!" John Henry shouted, his anger and fear consuming him.

"I told him he need to go back to the Wrash and tell his ho ass mom I'll be there later tonight."

John Henry lunged and punched Doomsday in the face. Immediately, he felt flurry of blows hit from all directions. He felt a hard crack on his head, and everything went black.

TRACK 10

STILLETTA JAMES WALKED INTO GURU'S. She knew about it from stories but had never been in person. Gibran was a legend. She wondered what he was like. She told herself she didn't go because she was too proud, but inside she knew she was nervous and afraid of how she would measure up to one of the greats. Meeting with John Henry was a good diversion for her thoughts and made it easier to step through the door.

The store wasn't anything special. It looked like someone's personal collection of stuff. Old media in boxes on tables. She had only seen a few in person before. At the front was a display case with similar media. It must have been special because of the separation, but it was hard to tell a notable difference. Stilletta James recognized some of the names, like Jay Z and Chance the Rapper, but others like Jean Grae and J Dilla were foreign to her.

The store looked empty. Nobody was behind the display counter. She leaned to look down the nearest aisle but didn't see anybody. Down on the table in front of her was a CD with a picture of two towers exploding. There were two people in the front. In the corner was a star with a woman in it with a gun over her shoulder. Something about the album cover seemed familiar but she couldn't place it.

"That CD was never released."

The voice behind her made her jump. She looked up to see a man standing behind the counter. She wondered how he got there without making a sound. He must have walked from one of the aisles. He had a tight beanie on his head with a black suede jacket and a white shirt underneath. The black of the jacket provided a contrast to the light brown color of his skin.

"The cover was too controversial at the time. It was set to drop right before September 11. The Coup changed their CD cover to a martini glass. It took the edge off a little bit, but the album still thumps. '5 Million Ways to Kill a CEO' is my jam. I remember seeing them in person too. They had a live funk band, while Boots Riley rapped. Nobody else was really doing that at the time except for the Roots. But both of them are some of the best of all time."

Stilletta James just stared at him and tried to digest what he just said. She had no idea what he was talking about, but it made her want to listen to the album. The twin tower explosion registered in her mind and that's what was nagging her about the album cover. Blacks having to worry about being associated with terrorism didn't make sense to her. She had always associated Whites with terrorism.

"I'll have to check it out," she said at last.

"For real. Don't sleep on that album," Gibran replied. "But you didn't come to hear me wax poetic about the old school. What you need homegirl?"

"I was supposed to meet John Henry here," she said.

Gibran's eyes narrowed with suspicion.

"You were going to meet John Henry….here?" Gibran said as he pointed to the counter. Gibran hadn't seen John Henry since his show. He had seen the streams and saw what happened. He didn't know what to make of it and wanted to talk with John Henry in person. This girl showing up at his shop before John Henry put him on guard.

"Yeah. After shit went down at the show, he and I scrambled out of there. He didn't have his SMiRK on and freaked out. I ran after him. He didn't stop until he was in the subway staircase. I wanted to know what he did with the eshirts. I tried to talk with him right then, but he was going crazy. He couldn't talk straight, and he kept thinking the Pats or an angry mob was gonna mirk him. He told me to meet him here today and then ran off into the subway tunnel. I fucking hate the subway. No way I was chasing after him."

"Have you seen the streams?" Gibran asked as he eyed Stilletta James.

"Yeah. How can you not? They're blastin that shit out everywhere. Haven't seen that kind of coverage in a while. John Henry here?"

"No queen. Been keepin' my eye out, but I haven't seen him."

It was Stilletta James' turn to be skeptical. Why would John Henry go out of his way to meet up with her on this side of the Pigeon line and then not show up? She knew he was tied to Gibran because of how he got his show at the Hive.

"You trying to play me? He's not in the back?"

"I said he ain't here queen. I'm too old to be fuckin around. He ain't here. Word is bond."

"Aiight gramps. Ease your coal. I'll chill for a bit then. Maybe he'll be here soon."

"Check out that CD then. Might learn something."

"I don't even know how to play this gramps."

"Gimme that shit," Gibran said and reached and grabbed it from her. He put it into the player behind the counter and pressed play.

Stilletta James waited through the whole album. She was in and out thinking about John Henry and everything that had happened since the night of the show to now. She remembered her visit to Commander Gates' station and her encounter with the Four Horseman. Then a thread started to form in her mind. The Four Horseman were in the front row at the Hive, even in the doctored version. They were also at the station with Commander Gates. Why were they at the show and then the station? Commander Gates said he was getting information from them, but what if them being at the show wasn't a coincidence? Then she remembered she had told Gates she was coming here to meet John Henry.

"Fuck!" she thought to herself.

She came back to reality. Gibran was looking for something else to play lost in thoughts of his own.

"Gibran, I think I know where he is," she said. "He's at the Pigeon Police station."

"*The* Pigeon Police station?" Gibran grimaced. "They'll fuck him up in there."

"I'ma head out maybe I can talk to Gates. I know him."

"You know that greasy pig?"

"I don't want to get into it," Stilletta James said avoiding having to own up why she really knows him. "Peace king. That album was brash though."

"Let me know if I can help," Gibran called out as the door swung shut.

* * *

Stilletta James wanted to get to the station as quick as she could. The options were a car or the subway. She pressed her watch and the route came up on her Ox. The subway was going to be the fastest way to get there at this time and it was less creds. She touched her watch again and headed down the stairs. Whenever she descended into the subway, she tried to breathe through her mouth only but every once in a while, dank air would make its way into her nose and she would feel her mouth water and gag enough to make her nauseous. She would inhale through her mouth and then blow out with force trying to ward off the bad smell from coming back, but it would always find its way back.

Her subway ride viewing was the same as it was for John Henry. The same streams played on repeat with the same heads spinning them. The more she watched the video the more she saw something at play with the Horseman. Why were they in the front row? They didn't like her, and they would be too big to watch an unknown smirk like John Henry, let alone be in the front row. It just didn't seem right.

She exited the subway at the Pigeon Police station stop. Getting to the surface, she took a deep inhale. The fresh air was welcome even if it was all in her head. The station was two blocks away. She didn't know what her plan was. She felt like there was something weird going on, but why would they set up John Henry a random smirk rapper? Would she walk in and ask Commander Gates if he had John Henry or would she be more demanding? She didn't have much leverage. She decided she would play it cool and just see what was going on.

A few hundred feet from the station, she looked up and something caught her eye. A person in a green SMiRK stepped out from the shadows across the street from the station. The green SMiRK caught her off guard, but then she remembered what Gates had said about the Graft. The man had something strapped around him, but she couldn't tell what it was.

Her muscles tightened and she stopped. She realized what was happening and ducked into a nearby doorway. From her hiding place she heard a shout.

"Power to the Fathers!"

The explosive wave burst past where she was standing, and broken glass flew with it. She staggered out from the doorway not knowing if it was safe but thinking she should help. She couldn't tell if her ears were ringing or if the sound was coming from emergency sirens. Everything felt quiet except the ringing. Then the noise came back and hit her in the head sending her reeling again. There were screams at the station and people running every direction like ants in a panic.

As she limped forward, she happened to look down the alley next to the station. A green hooded figure was dragging another person to a car. Her mind and eyes came together and focused for the first time since the explosion. It was John Henry.

"Hey!" Stilletta James screeched. "Hey!"

She couldn't find any other words. They were not close, and the figure was going to get John Henry to the car before she would even be close. She started their way anyway trying to build speed. Her body and legs felt like jelly. Her brain was still trying to unscramble the events and piece everything together, but her adrenaline was pumping through her pushing her to make decisions. Just as she started to run, John Henry disappeared into the car.

A third green figure jumped out of the car with the same equipment as the one who had just blown himself up. She skidded to a halt. He took a step toward her and she turned to run.

She barely heard his "Power to the Fathers" before she felt the explosion and flew forward to the ground.

She rolled over and sucked in air. Looking up into the narrow line of sky the alley formed, she sucked in another gasp. Her body kept gasping air and she couldn't do anything but feel her heart race and her head pulse.

After what felt like an hour she rolled over and her hands and knees. She crawled to the wall beside her and used it to pull herself up. Vertigo struck her and she had to close her eyes as she propped herself against the wall. Her mind was still spinning but it felt better in darkness. She slid along the wall with her eyes closed.

At this point, the ringing in her ears felt permanent. She had even more questions than she started with, but she couldn't even walk straight let alone think straight. She didn't want to deal with the police or anybody asking her questions, so she staggered off down the street.

* * *

Stilletta James pushed through the door of Guru's and limped in. The pain in her head had reduced to a steady pulse and the ringing in her ears had gone down. Her side ached and she was confident she had broken at least a couple of ribs. Her dark clothes were covered in dust and probably some blood.

"What the fuck happened to you?" Stilletta James heard Gibran ask her. Without waiting for her reply, he realized, "Oh shit, you were there. The streams went crazy about an hour ago. You alright? Come here and sit down."

Gibran guided her to a chair, where she slumped down.

"They fucking got him," she croaked out.

"Who got who?" he asked not understanding.

"The Graft," she said again in her hoarse voice. She took a deep breath trying to stay calm. "They blew that shit up and fucking took him out. John Henry. They fucking took him."

"What do you mean they took him?"

"They fucking took him from the police station! The whole bombing was a setup to get him out of there. I saw them put him into the car and then the second bomb went off. Fuck!" she shouted and massaged her temples as she sat in the chair.

"Where do you think they took him?"

"How the fuck should I know? The Wrash? The fucking Graft Cave?"

Gibran went silent, then he walked down and started messing with a tablet on the counter.

"He had to give me his address in the Wrash so I could get him his visa. It's just him and his mom. Maybe you could start with her."

"Us? Go to the Wrash, while this Graft shit is going on? Are you fucking kidding me?"

"Nah, I don't leave the store. I stopped a long time ago."

"So, you're saying just me go to the Wrash then? And talk with the mom of this guy who is all over the streams?"

"If they kill him, that's on you. Or worse, what if they use him to kill more Blacks? Maybe his eshirt thing got him into some trouble and that's why the Pats and the Graft are after him."

She hadn't thought any of this had to do with the eshirts, but it made sense. "Why else would both sides be tracking him down? They didn't care about his raps."

The picture of her brother pushed its way into her mind, and she remembered John Henry laying knocked out on stage helpless.

"Ok I'll fucking do it. Only so nobody else gets hurt though."

"Before you go, you should probably take these," Gibran said as he handed her a bag.

She opened it and saw four little tablets in a bag with some chords.

"What are these?" she asked.

"They're phones from back in the day. It's what he used to do the thing with the shirts. I don't know if they can be any help, but you might as well take them. Just in case." He also thought he would rather not have them in the store if other people came looking for them.

"You owe me next time I'm back."

He nodded. She took the bag and limped out.

TRACK 11

JOHN HENRY WAS BEING LED through a dark hallway. He walked on his own, but someone was next to him guiding him. The hall was too dark to see who it was. He didn't have his SMiRK on. They came into a room with windows and the light hit his eyes giving him a sharp pain to accompany the ringing in his ears.

After a few seconds, he could see they were in a warehouse of some sort. It had high windows along the walls that let sun into the room in a line. He panicked for a second thinking the sun might be hitting him, but with a quick scan realized he was well out of the light. He was still walking and the person guiding him was in a green SMiRK.

Then everything came rushing back.

He had been in a room at the police station. The Pigeon Police were interrogating him. He had been in there for a couple of hours it seemed. He was trying to keep his cool and not say anything, but they were peppering questions with punches to his face and baton blows to the body. At one point a person left because he remembered the door opening and closing and that's when everything accelerated.

The door opened and someone undid his handcuffs to the chair and rushed him out. He made it a few steps out of the door before collapsing. Two men in green SMiRKs dragged him down a hallway and out a door.

While he was trying to figure out what was going on, he heard and felt an explosion nearby and his head reeled and spun, and he blacked out.

Each step hurt for John Henry. The police had broken at least one of his ribs. His right eye throbbed a little bit and he had a hard time focusing.

He and the green SMiRK person kept walking.

"Graft?" John Henry rasped.

"How'd you know?" Robert Graft IV responded with a trace of sarcasm, although it was hard to know for sure as he was breathing heavy. "Let's save the questions until we make it to the room."

They finished crossing the warehouse floor and entered through a door into a small office. Robert Graft IV led John Henry in, and half shoved half dropped him on to a ragged brown couch. Robert Graft IV continued around a desk and plopped into a high-backed leather office chair. There were no windows to this room just white fluorescent lighting. Robert Graft IV pulled off the hood and goggles of his SMiRK and kicked his legs up on the desk.

John Henry had a hard time taking in what he was looking at. John Henry couldn't remember the last time he saw white skin in person if ever. Robert Graft IV wasn't just white, his skin seemed almost translucent. His hair, eyebrows, and eyelashes were all blonde and his eyes were red. John Henry felt like he was looking at a monster from a horror movie.

"Didn't I tell you?" Robert Graft IV said.

"Tell me what?" John Henry replied, not really knowing if he was looking for an answer.

"The Pigeon Police. The Blacks. They don't give a fuck about you. They were going to kill you in that room. All for what? So, they could stop you from doing your eshirt trick. Or use it themselves? Shit, they wouldn't even know what to fucking do with it."

John Henry didn't answer. He revisited the events of the day before. He had risked going to Guru's out of ambition. He hadn't thought Stilletta James would have given him up to the Pigeon Police. Why hadn't he thought that? The potential to be famous had clouded his judgement. It had led him right into the hands of the Pigeon Police. Stilletta James had set up the whole encounter. She was probably friends with the Four Horseman from the Hive. Did she set up the attack on stage too? Probably. Was Gibran in on it too? Did he push John Henry to perform just to get caught? His head was spinning with the possibilities. The thought of Gibran betraying him tightened his stomach. Even though it was a short time, John Henry had thought he connected with Gibran. He never really had a father in his life, and it felt good to look up to someone. Now that was shattered. Maybe?

Robert Graft IV chuckled and John Henry looked up.

"I can see it your face," Graft said. "You honestly didn't see this coming. Don't you watch the streams? When is the last time you saw Blacks doing anything for Whites?"

"I don't know," John Henry mumbled. "I guess I thought it was different. Different for me."

"Different for you? Johnny boy, you really are dumb. They have the power! You don't just give that away. It has to be wrestled away. That's what we're about. The Graft. We're here for equality. Bringing Blacks and Whites equal with each other. Getting enough power for us to let society run fairly like it was meant to under the Founding Fathers."

"If you're for equality and just for your share of power, why all the bombs? The killing? They'll never give up power that way."

"John, you just don't see it do you? It's all lies. We don't kill or bomb. It's them. They alter the streams. Provide the heads with spin. Next thing you have is the 'Evil Graft,'" Robert Graft IV brought up his pale hands to air quote the last words. "If they can control the narrative, we'll never get the power. We need to take the narrative in our own hands. Show people were all the same on the inside. Just humans trying to make it. Picture it John. Blacks and Whites walking down streets with no SMiRKs and no Pigeon Police. Just humans living. Make society great together."

Graft's words diminished the ringing in his ears as John Henry started to picture what Graft was talking about. What would it be like to walk without a SMiRK? To not live in fear every day? Not being hungry in the Wrash?

"And this is where you come in," Graft's words pulled John Henry from his daydream. "You have this technology. This medium that has been suppressed and controlled by Blacks for the last 20 years. You've figured it out. How to unlock it. And you know what that means? We can take back the narrative. We can get our message of equality out to everyone. To show everyone what the Graft is about. Equality. Not all Blacks are driven by power. They'll see our message and help. It won't be easy, but it will be a start. A steppingstone."

"You think you can do all that with what I got?" John Henry asked, skeptical that his shirt trick could change the masses and solve the environmental crisis.

"I do!" Graft said with a smile on his face. "Instead of doing something musical like you did, we can broadcast to everyone, everywhere. It will be like when my great grandpa did Presidential addresses to reach the nation. Great unifying speeches."

John Henry didn't remember ever hearing anything positive about President Graft, but he was thinking about hope and change and didn't dwell on what he didn't know. But then it all came tumbling down in his mind. He felt the pockets of his SMiRK. Nothing. He reached for his wrists and he had no watch devices there either.

"Graft-," John Henry started.

"Call me Bobby," Graft interjected.

"Ok, Bobby, I have bad news," John Henry looked down at his hands. "The way I control the eshirts is through old phones and my watch device. I don't have either of those things though and I need both. They must be back at the police station."

Robert Graft IV looked at him with a smirk and then pulled a bag on the table.

"You mean these things?" he asked as he dumped the bag out revealing the phone and the chipped watches he had been wearing at the time.

"You got them!" John Henry shouted. "How did you get them?"

"How did we get them? How are we here Johnny boy," Graft said opening his arms to the room. "We have people everywhere. Also, it doesn't hurt when you have credits to spare. When my dad left this world. Rest in peace. He left me with a few credits, and you can get anything done with a few credits. So, are you going to show me how to use these things or not?"

"If it gets the Pigeon Pats off my back," he hesitated. "Fuck it, let's do it." John Henry was ready to make his SMiRKless dream happen.

Graft's eyes narrowed and his smile faded for just a second as he heard John Henry's words, but then returned as soon as they had gone as John Henry got up and walked to the desk forgetting the pain in his body.

John Henry powered on the phone and the wrist device. He went over it with Robert Graft IV for the next couple of hours. His excitement guided him, and he made sure Graft knew about all of the features on how to use it. They sampled a few shirts to make sure it worked. Graft even asked him questions he hadn't expected about using the phones to turn on other electronics. John Henry hadn't tried it before, but he messed with it until he figured it out. He was able to get the watch-phone combo to turn on a nearby stream tablet. Finally, John Henry's adrenaline for the future wore off and the pain came pulsing back in his ribs and his head.

"Bobby, do you have a safe place to stay?" John Henry asked knowing he couldn't go back to his place now that he was a fugitive from the Pigeon Police. "I feel like shit. I'm gonna need to pass out soon."

"Yes. I do. I thought of that. We have a set up just for you up on the second story."

Robert Graft IV led John Henry to the door and opened it for him. The warehouse was dark now that it was night except for a few dim lights lining the walls. John Henry stepped out looking for the stairs to the next level. Then he felt a cloth around his mouth and his body jerk as an arm grabbed him around the neck. That was the last thing he remembered before he blacked out.

John Henry felt weightless before he felt the pain in his ribs and his armpits. Then he opened his eyes and understood why. He looked down at his feet dangling. The ground was probably about ten feet away. He looked up and saw the rope that went under his armpits lead up to the rafters, then it continued back down and was tied off against the wall. He struggled and twisted and turned. His arms were tied around his torso, so he couldn't reach the rope behind him. He kept moving until he was sweating and breathing hard.

"Fuck!" he shouted in frustration.

"I wouldn't twist too much."

John Henry heard the voice and craned his neck to see who it was. He couldn't see until Robert Graft IV walked in front of him.

"Bobby! They got me mirked up here. Help me out king. The ropes on the wall over there. How did you get away from the Pats?"

"The Pats?" Robert Graft IV looked at him with a quizzical expression. "They were here?"

"Yeah, king! Look! They got me mirked up here."

"Oh Johnny, so smart with the gadgets but so naïve."

"What are you talking about Bobby?" John Henry asked, but then it hit him.

"Aww now you see. Just a little too late."

"Why?" asked John Henry. "I gave you what you asked for. I showed you how to use the phone and the eshirts."

"Did you though Johnny? I came to you the first time. I told you about the movement and you thought I was crazy. You didn't listen to me."

"What the fuck are you talking about Graft? I met you one time before. What'd you want me to do? Risk going to jail to hang out with a fucking terrorist?"

"Terrorist? Me? You tried to do your thing with the Blacks. You wanted hip hop. Rap music. How did they treat you? They fucking beat you and put you in jail and I'm the terrorist? You're not down for the movement. You're not proud to be White. You're just another Black bastard anyway."

"Not proud to live in fear with a fucking sheet on my head everywhere I go? Fuck you king. I was trying to be better."

"Well shucks, I guess we agree there, because I am going to make the world better, but it will be a little late for you. Thanks to you for showing me how to use these," Graft held up the phone and watch. "It's finally time for me to even the odds. Take the power back. This phone, your phone, will bring the Whites back. Just a small click and BOOM! Just a little nukey nuke to block the sun out for good. We'll be able to come out and settle the score. No more SMiRKs. No more hiding in the shadows. Put the power back in the hands of the descendants of the founding fathers."

"You're fucking washed, king!" John Henry spat at Graft. "You'll kill everyone doing that."

"Maybe I will," Robert Graft IV winked at him and turned and walked out.

TRACK 12

STILLETTA JAMES COULDN'T BRING HERSELF to use the subway again so she had taken a car. Subways were the only vehicles that crossed the Pigeon Line, so she had to get out to cross the checkpoint on foot. Because of the bombing at the police station earlier in the day, the agents at the gates were on edge with their guns out instead of their normal position slung across the shoulder. They were not letting Whites cross the Pigeon Line to the Black side. Only Whites returning from work were being let back through to get home. Stilletta James stood out in the line of white SMiRKs waiting to be processed.

Stilletta James had never been to Wrashtown. She had only heard stories of what it was like and seen footage from the streams. Black women being raped by White men was a common story, usually followed by a mob mirking on the other side of the Pigeon Line. As she got closer to the front of the line, she could smell her sweat. Her heartbeat had picked up too.

"What the fuck are you doing?" the agent asked.

"I'm going to the Wrash," Stilletta James mumbled. His question adding to her nerves.

"You know were not letting anyone back on this side. The shit that went down today has everything on lock down. Probably won't open it back up for a couple of days"

"I know," she said, but she hadn't known. She was ready to turn around when pictures of her brother flashed into her mind, followed by the image of John Henry being dragged from the police station, and the man in the green SMiRK exploding. She'll never be able to erase the image from her memory. Just thinking of the explosion brought the ringing back to her ears. She had to get to John Henry's mom to save him and maybe stop the Graft.

"You have a place to stay?" the agent asked offering one more way out.

"I do," she said as he scanned the visa paperwork she had from Gibran with his Ox.

It must have checked out because he let her through. Dozens of Whites were congregating at the gate on the other side. The anger from the lockdown was electric on this side of the line. A lot of Whites wouldn't be able to make it to their jobs the next morning. Most of them were just hanging on with their credits. They couldn't afford to miss work.

She didn't know where she was going but she knew she couldn't stay there. She was the only Black this side of the gate and she didn't want to be on the wrong side of one of the streams she was thinking of earlier.

Stilletta James scanned the address with her Ox and started to follow the path to John Henry's apartment. It was a thirty-minute walk away. She didn't trust taking a car.

Project housing buildings made up the bulk of Wrashtown. Businesses were few and far between, an occasional corner store. Most things were made in the 3D and everything else came from outside. She walked by bodies lying on the ground in corners and alleys. Stilletta James couldn't tell if some of them were passed out or dead.

With one block to go, she looked behind her and realized there were three SMiRK clad figures following her. Stilletta James had been so caught up with everything around her she lost her anxiety. The three figures put a lump in her throat and her mouth felt dry. She could smell her sweat again and feel her heart quicken in her chest. The Ox showed her three minutes to arrival.

She turned into the next project building. She had to go up to the fourth floor. The elevators were broken as she passed them to the stairs. Probably for the best, if she stopped to wait the figures would catch up with her. She opened the stair door. As soon as it closed, she ran up the stairs. She had to make it up four flights and then find the door. What would she do if his mom wasn't there? She was on the second flight when she heard the stair door open and then shut. She could hear the shuffle of feet and SMiRKs running up the stairs. She kept pace and bound two steps at a time.

She sprinted through the fourth story door to a long hallway. Her Ox pointed her to the door at the end of the hall. The stairs door closed behind her as she made it to John Henry's apartment. She pressed the pad. Nothing. She pressed it again, a couple of times. Nothing.

"Come on, come on," Stilletta James whispered to herself.

She hit it with her fist and heard a chirp. She wasn't sure if she broke it or if it did something else. Then she heard the stairs door open. The three figures poured through. She turned to face them trying to figure out what she would do.

"Who are you?" a voice said from behind her.

She spun around and saw a black skinned woman standing in front of her. This stunned her and she didn't know what to say, then she remembered the figures behind her and did another turn. They were still coming although they had slowed down.

The woman stepped in front of her pushing her back into the door with her arm.

"Get outta here," she said with a black baton in her hand low to her side. The figures kept coming but slower.

"I said get the fuck outta here," she pressed something on the baton, and it emitted a static electrical noise and the tip lit blue. She struck it against the wall with a sharp electrical crack. The figures stopped. She backed up into her door forcing Stilletta James into the apartment, but not taking her eyes off of the figures. Once in the threshold enough, she pressed the door button and it slid closed.

The room was dim. Stilletta James' eyes worked to adjust. The blue light at the end of the baton maintained a steady glow as the woman at the door turned to Stilletta James.

"Who are you?" she asked. "What are you doing here?"

"Thanks for saving me from those smirks," Stilletta James exhaled ignoring the question.

"You watch your mouth in my house," the woman said as she brought the baton up and pointed the blue tip at Stilletta James. Stilletta James wobbled back out of the woman's reach and almost fell over a couch.

"What are you doing here?" the woman repeated. "I don't want any trouble queen."

"I'm looking for John Henry," Stilletta James said, figuring honesty was her best course of action with the baton in her face.

The woman stiffened but kept the baton up. She didn't respond.

"Have you seen the streams? Do you know what happened?" Stilletta James followed up.

Stilletta James could see the tears welling up in the woman's eyes confirming she had. The woman shook her head and lowered the baton.

"What are you doing here?" she repeated for the third time replacing the menacing tone with a defeated one.

Stilletta James told John Henry's mom the story of the Hive, which had been blasted all over the streams. She seemed familiar with most of the details, but it was hard for Stilletta James to read her. She was quiet throughout the story until Stilletta James recanted the events at the police station.

"Why were you at the police station?" his mom asked.

"I was waiting for him at Guru's, the shop across the Pigeon Line, where he'd been hanging out."

John Henry's mom interrupted.

"I know what Guru's is, why were you there?"

"I was waiting to meet John Henry like we agreed but then realized it was a setup. The Pigeon Pats wanted him. Gates had gamed me into giving him information on John Henry. I was headed back to ask him what he wanted John Henry for. I think it had all been a plan to get him to the station, but why did they want him? He was just rapping. He ain't no terrorist."

John Henry's mom stiffened when she heard Gates' name but kept listening.

"Of course he's not a terrorist, but the Pigeon Police don't care. That's not what they're here for. They're here to spread their own terror. Can't have people, especially White people, breaking the rules especially ones with credit contract impacts. They got John because he was playing with fire. You can't let that slide."

John Henry's mom talked about the Pigeon Police as if she were recollecting something she had talked about many times before.

"If you're worried about their terror, why are you living on this side of the Pigeon Line. You're Black. You and John Henry could be living on the other side."

His mom let out a slow chuckle.

"You think I'm living here by choice queen? Come on girl, you think someone would live here by choice?"

Stilletta James didn't understand or respond. His mom went on.

"You think you know Gates? I know Gates. I was with him. Fought alongside of him. Rounding up Whites. Sending them to the Wrash. Fucking Whites had held us down for so long. Fought so hard to keep their privilege. Keep their power. Couldn't just let them get off clean. It was our time. If only the Flip were that easy?"

"One day I looked in the mirror and saw a subtle black line along my neck. I didn't think anything of it until I saw a few more show up on my hands and legs. I went to the doctor. He had never seen anything like it. Thought maybe it was the sun."

Stilletta James finally noticed her skin was a little different. She could see several dark lines along her neck and arms.

"I couldn't accept that. If it was the Sun, then who was I? What was I doing? I didn't care that I was dying slowly. Everything I was doing was going against what I was becoming. I hid it from my friends, from my husband. Just kept on fighting, moving. Making things 'right'," she said the last part with a sarcastic emphasis and air quotes.

"But I couldn't fight it forever. I started getting weaker and weaker, until one day I passed out in the sun. My husband took me to the doctor. The doctor confirmed what he had thought all along. It was the sun.

"That was the end of it for me. You think you know love until you feel the hate. Then the darkness comes even quicker. He threw me and John out of the house. John was only two years old, but his dad didn't want any chance of having a White child ruin his ambition.

"He had goals. He had plans. He had hate. He wanted to lead the Pigeon Police. He can't have a White child and do that. I haven't seen Gates in 20 years. He got what he wanted. I guess he did the right thing."

The revelation was staggering for Stilletta James.

Had Gates known he was interrogating his own son? Framing him with streams and making him disappear?

She had always wondered why he didn't have a family. Why he spent so much time with youth in the community. Did he feel regret? Was he trying to pay off a debt? Or was he trying to build something he would never have?

"What's your plan" his mom broke her thoughts.

"You were my plan," Stilletta James said. "You and these phones."

She dumped the remaining phones from Gibran on the table. John Henry's mom picked one up. She moved it around with her hands and then pressed a button on it. The screen lit up.

"I haven't seen one of these in a long time."

She used her fingers to scroll through the screen.

"I don't know how to use them," Stilletta James said as his mom continued to play with the phone.

"I have an idea," she responded. "There used to be an app on here you could use to find another phone. If John Henry linked these phones up, we would be able to see it. Here we go. I got it! You see this phone?"

His mom pointed to an icon of a phone on the map.

"That's where the phone is," she said. "That's a couple of miles from here near Graft Park."

"The Graft!" Stilletta James exclaimed with anger in her voice. "I gotta go find him. I can't let the Graft kill him or anybody else."

John Henry's mom eyed her not knowing what to think.

"You can't go out without a SMiRK though. Someone will come after you like they did on the way here."

She left and came back with a SMiRK.

"Here you go," she handed it to Stilletta James.

Stilletta James took it and looked at it.

"You'll have to wear it. It's the only way. But we can deal with that in the morning. No way you're going out there this late. It will protect you from the sun but it don't make you invincible."

"But what about John Henry? He's with the Graft. We can't just leave him with them," Stilletta James said.

"Girl, what is your name?"

"Henrietta," Stilletta James replied with her real name. It surprised even her coming out. "But I go by Stilletta James." She added in a low voice and trailed off almost like she thought it was a silly nickname all of a sudden.

"Henrietta, I love my son. I want him back and safe. But do you think one person, even if they are *the* Stilletta James, is gonna make it through the Wrash in the middle of the night, and I'm assuming it is your first time in the Wrash, to confront the Graft and save my John? Nah queen. I tell John all of the time. You gotta be smarter than them. You gotta think queen. Going with the stream and the hype is gonna get you killed. Your best shot is going to be in the day when you'll fit in with all of the other SMiRKs no questions asked. Even then, ain't no small thing, but queen I respect your craft so maybe we're lucky tomorrow."

Stilletta James didn't speak. John Henry's mom emanated a powerful calm. It made her feel a little giddy inside to get the nod to her lyrics from this woman. Stilletta James wondered who this woman really was.

"You're right." Stilletta James said as she gathered the SMiRK up in her arms. "What about you? What's your name?"

"Simone," she responded.

TRACK 13

STILLETTA JAMES WALKED DOWN THE street with the SMiRK on. She had to look like everyone else so she couldn't just half ass it. Each step in the kit pulled her in a new way. She doubted she would ever get used to it. She wouldn't have been able to put it on without help from Simone. There were so many straps and buckles.

They had talked all night. Simone told her stories of before the Flip. Stories from her childhood. How Blacks were treated. How they were making progress until Robert Graft was elected. That's when it all fell apart. What progress Blacks thought they had made was rolled back when Whites felt their privilege start to slip. Things felt like they had reversed a hundred years over night. Whites grasping at their power. Government officials facilitating housing policies that left Black families reeling. Police officers killing Black civilians with no recourse. This last-ditch effort by Whites to maintain power drove the ugliness of the Flip. Blacks got the power and centuries of rage ignited a racial powder keg.

Stilletta James had read and learned about it in school but hearing about it from someone who was there made it different. Made it feel more real.

Stilletta James probably would have fed her anger all night if it weren't for the rest of Simone's story. How she became the very thing she fought against. Watching her life crumble before her eyes. Being thrown back to the Wrash by her friends and family.

Except she wasn't bitter. She talked about it with a longing look in her eyes, but the fire came back when she talked about John Henry. Teaching him. Watching him grow. Maybe the youth could change the world.

Stilletta James shook herself from the previous night's conversation. She looked at the map on the phone. The little phone icon they had found yesterday had gone from black to grey. She didn't know what that meant but stayed her course.

In the SMiRK nobody gave her a second thought. She melted into the crowd. A far throw from her jet-black outfits she usually wore on the street.

* * *

John Henry had been hanging for hours. His body ached. The beating from the police station combined with the slow pull of the ropes pulsed a dull pain through his body with epicenters around his armpits and ribs.

The sun had risen a few hours ago. He watched the beams through the windows stretch across the floor with time. The rays had hit his feet about a half an hour ago. His right arm would be the first exposed skin to see the light.

He had been hanging so long it was a little anticlimactic. The fear of being mirked had his adrenaline pumping when he first woke up after talking with Robert Graft IV, but his fear gave way to the slow rhythm of the pain.

Now he was just waiting. An almost curious anxiety building.

Would the sun even affect him? His skin was darker. He assumed darker than most whites, but truth be told he hadn't really seen others out of their SMiRKs before. He knew his mom only got sick after prolonged exposure. She had told him his dad was Black too. Maybe he was Black after all? Maybe nothing would happen?

The sun hit his fingertips. It felt warm, but he didn't feel anything else. A few minutes went by. His whole hand was in the light now. Nothing. His anxiety started to give way to a growing joy. The warmth of the sun was warming his heart.

He started to smile. Chuckled to himself. He was going to beat this.

Then he felt it. It was different from the warmth. Different from the slow pain he was already feeling. It started out as a small tingle in his fingertips but got louder and louder. It didn't feel like being burned more like the molecules in his hand had sped up and were out of control. What he imagined a microwave might feel like.

The feeling crept up his arm at a slow pace. It eclipsed his fingers and was moving into his hand. In a few more minutes his whole lower arm felt on fire.

* * *

It had taken Stilletta longer to get to the location than she had anticipated. She couldn't walk as fast in the SMiRK. She was doing her best not to stand out, which meant taking her time and walking at a normal pace. Wading through a sea of SMiRKs took some getting used to as well. She was raised to think that they were all terrorists. The mundaneness over their morning routine made them feel harmless and normal. It was clear they were just trying to get to their jobs or back home. Just normal. Trying to survive. The thousands of people in SMiRKs still spooked her. It felt like she was walking upstream against a river of ghosts.

She could see the windows high up lining the side of the building, but they were too high for her to get into the building. She circled the building a couple of times before she spotted a door with a glass window in it. She broke through it with a rock and was able to open the door.

There wasn't much outside light getting in, but once her eyes adjusted, she was able to make out the corridor in front of her. She took a step and hesitated. It didn't feel like anyone was here, but the Graft had kidnapped John Henry. Was this where they were? Were they guarding him? She had no way of knowing and continued to take each step with caution.

After ten minutes of slow walking, she made it to a door with a faint stream of light shining around it. She opened it without the care she had been taking with each step and the sun from the high windows hit her in the face. The contrast from the dark room she was just in put spots in her eyes. It took a few seconds to adjust. She could tell she was in a large empty warehouse but didn't see much more than that.

On the second scan back through she saw him hanging. The sun was covering his whole right arm. Something about his arm didn't look right from where she was standing, but she couldn't place it. His eyes and his face were locked in a still grimace. The sun would be on his face in a few minutes. Was he already dead?

"John Henry!" she shouted up at him.

His eyes shot open. It took him a moment to spot her. His face was tired. His whole body hung like a rag doll.

"Help me," he croaked. "My arm…it's almost at my face."

She followed the rope back to the wall and was going to run over and untie it, when she realized where he was hanging. The sun was shining on the ground right underneath him. If she lowered him down his face would be exposed to the sun. She didn't know how long it would take to affect him, but she didn't want to chance it.

"Untie the rope…it's on the wall," he said and lifted his head in an attempt to point to the rope.

"I can see the rope! Give me a second," she snapped back at him, more frustrated with the problem then with John Henry. She started unbuckling the straps on her SMiRK. It took her longer than she anticipated.

"Here we go king. Pray to your god," she said as she threw the SMiRK at him. It hit him in the arm and fell to the ground.

"What are you doing? Just get me down," he said in a drawn out and exasperated tone.

She didn't respond but threw the SMiRK a second time. Again, it fell to the ground. The sun's rays were at John Henry's shoulder.

She threw it a third time and it went over his head and stayed. Stilletta James could hear muffled speech from John Henry but couldn't make it out. He was probably cursing her and wondering what she was doing.

Stilletta James tied the excess rope around her waist so John Henry wouldn't drop to the ground when she untied him. Once the knot was loose, the rope cinched around her waist and John Henry dropped a couple of inches.

The rope continued to pull at her waist as she walked toward him. Each step lowered John Henry with a soft jerk. He hit the ground after about five more steps and the bite of the rope disappeared from Stilletta James' waist. She dragged him to the shade and plopped down. Her chest heaved from exerting herself and sweat beaded on her forehead. She heard the muffled speech again. She leaned over and tugged the SMiRK off of John Henry's face.

"Can you untie me?" he forced the words out between breaths. The pain in his ribs had become more apparent now that he was lying on his side and his blood was pumping.

Stilletta James undid the ropes around his armpits and realized his hands were tied at the waist too. Then she noticed what was different about his right arm. It was black. An unnatural black. The true black of dead skin.

"John Henry," Stilletta James murmured. "Your arm."

He rolled his body and sat up using his left hand. He looked down at his right arm. It was black and lifeless.

"Can you move it?" she asked. "Does it hurt?"

"No," he responded. His shoulder moved a little bit, but the arm refused to budge. He used his left hand to lift up his right shirt sleeve. There was a line where the black skin ended, and his brown skin begun. It almost looked like someone had tattooed his entire arm. He just stared at it. John Henry stoop up awkwardly using his good hand. Stilletta James could tell he was trying to move it. He poked it with his other hand.

"I don't think it works anymore. I've never known anyone who has been half mirked before. I guess my mom is close. I wonder if it will spread," he asked to no one in particular. "Thanks," he said added after a few minutes of silence. Both of them were thinking about his arm and his mom.

"That could have been my face. What an idiot. Fucking Graft."

Stilletta James went stiff. She had forgotten about the Graft.

"Are they here?" she said as she stood up and looked around.

"I don't think so. He left a while ago. Before the sun came up. He's fucking crazy. He's going to blow up the city.

"He's going to blow up the city? That fucker just don't quit."

"He thinks it will fix everything. He's just going to make it worse. We have to stop him."

"How you gonna do that king? He's got a bomb."

"I showed him how to use the phone to turn things on and off. I didn't realize what he was asking for at the time, not until I was hanging up there. I think I can stop him if I get close enough. I think talking to the police is out. They think I'm with him and won't listen to me if I told them. That and even if they believed me, I don't think they would be able to get close enough before he would set off the bomb. Do you have the phones?"

"Yeah, how did you know?"

"That was the only way you could have found me. We'll need to use them to find him and then shut the bomb down. We'll need to pick up some things from Guru's first. I saw some things there that could help give us a little more range."

"John Henry," Stilletta James said. "I'm sorry. I didn't set you up. I mean

I was talking to the police, but I…" she went silent. She didn't know how to explain.

"I didn't mean for it to happen like this," she finished as she looked away and let her voice trail off.

He looked at her and then he looked down at his arm.

TRACK 14

THE PLAN WAS THE TWO would split up. John Henry would head to Guru's to fill Gibran in and pick up a few extra electronics to help him shut down the bomb. Stilletta James would head to the police station and tell them she found John Henry mirked in a warehouse in the Wrash. Hopefully, thinking he was dead would keep the pigeon police distracted for Stilletta James and John Henry to get a jump on tracking down Robert Graft IV.

Stilletta James needed a strategy to get out of the Wrash. To her dismay, she had to put the SMiRK back on. The easiest way across the Pigeon Line was through the subway. The entrances weren't manned like they were on the surface. You had to scan your credentials to get through. The gates opened fine when Stilletta James scanned her watch and her Ox, even though she was in a full SMiRK. Once she got across the Pigeon Line, she ditched the SMiRK and climbed to the surface.

When Stilletta James neared the police station, officers with assault rifles clogged the streets. There were several stationed on corners starting several blocks out. It felt a little heavy handed and impotent to her at this point, knowing that Robert Graft IV was somewhere else in the City.

The vision of the bombing replayed in her mind and she felt her stomach get queasy. The two green SMiRK men had blown themselves up right in front of her. She would have nightmares about it for months to come. Maybe forever.

She sat down to take a moment and turned the streams on. They were focused on the bombing from the day before. They showed several different angles of the bombings, but none were like being there in person. They didn't provide the shockwave or the nausea Stilletta James felt.

The streams recapped with a picture of John Henry and footage from the show the other night. They alluded to that night being the first step in a greater Graft plot. Stilletta James felt her coal heat up. Her time with Simone and John Henry had shifted her heart if not on Whites at least the two of them. But then they showed a picture of Robert Graft IV. His face was unnaturally white with blood red eyes. The fire in her chest went from one end of the spectrum to the other with the full weight of her disdain for the Graft pumping into her soul. This thing was trying to bring back a time of hate and disregard for human life. All for what? The privilege to live without consequence. To be above the law and suppress those looking for equality.

Stilletta James shook herself from those thoughts. She had to get to Commander Gates to keep their plan in action. As she walked to the station her nerves started to build. She knew she wasn't wearing a SMiRK but the fact that she had one on for the last few hours felt like it left a permanent imprint with her. At any moment she felt one of the guards could stop her and ask her what she has been doing and she would be caught. She had to get her pulse under control before screaming her plan out of frustration.

She made it to the station. Everyone was running everywhere, and nobody was focused on the woman in dark black clothing. She could have been a shadow flitting by.

The receptionist robot was turned off and a pigeon police officer manned the counter. They were taking every precaution to prevent another attack. Exerting their will to prevent lighting from striking twice.

"I'm here to see Commander Gates," Stilletta James announced to the police officer.

The officer looked Stilletta James up and down.

"He's busy," the officer said.

"Tell him it's Henrietta," Stilletta James told her.

"What part of busy don't you understand? Do you know what just happened? You watched the streams? He's going to be busy for a while."

"Just send him a note, he'll come, you'll see," Stilletta James countered. She wasn't going to have this officer ruin the plan.

"He's busy. I suggest you leave and come back. It's not going to be any time soon."

Stilletta James decided for a different approach. It might bring more attention, but it was probably her only chance at this point.

"I have information on the Graft," Stilletta James said.

The face of the officer changed from uncaring. It flashed to angry and then turned and to look Stilletta James in the eye.

"What information?" the officer asked.

"I'll tell Commander Gates. Tell him it's Henrietta."

"I'm going to need more information to pull him away."

"Tell him it's about John Henry and Robert Graft IV."

The officer wasn't sure if she was being serious at this point or not but wasn't willing to second guess it and feel the brunt of it later. She walked off. Disregarding known terrorist information would be career ending.

The officer returned a few minutes later with a sour look on their face. Stilletta James took it as a good sign.

"He said he'll see you. Follow me."

The officer turned and walked back down the hall without waiting for Stilletta James to follow. They arrived at Commander Gates office and the officer stopped, waited for her to enter, and then walked off without any further communication.

"Well, well, well, Henrietta," Commander Gates said in a snarky tone. "I wasn't expecting you back here."

She winced at the sound of her real name. It reminded her of the tone her teachers used to take with her when she was busy writing rhymes in school instead of paying attention.

"But here I am," she said. "You know you right though. You a fucking snake. Played me to get to John Henry."

"It's my job. I'm here to protect the people from the Graft. From the Whites."

"You fucking blind king. Have you been to the Wrash lately? Those ghosts out there just shuffling trying to make it. Trying to hold on. The only one keeping the Graft alive is you. Who do you think they cling to hate? You and all the other Pigeon Pats. You ain't protecting shit. You flipped on Simone the minute she was a threat to your own ambition and now you're trying to take down your own son? Well they fucking mirked him so the next time you see the Graft maybe tell them thanks you wrash mothafucker."

Commander Gates flinched at the mention of Simone, but his face remained stoic and unemotional at the mention of John Henry.

"How long have you known?"

He didn't respond.

"You've known the whole time? You were trying to take out your own son?"

"I don't have a son. He was born to die. His own people brought it on themselves. That's one less Graft and one step closer to achieving the goal."

"Are you listening to yourself king? His people? You are his people! The only thing that makes him Whiter than me or you is the sun. You fucking washed king."

His face remained ice cold. Stilletta James' words were falling on rock. It would take a deeper movement of the plates to triumph over his geology.

"Well if you want to see him, he's in the Wrash in a warehouse near Graft park. You can check the vids to find the exact one."

"Thanks for the information, Henrietta," Gates said the snark was back in his tone. "And if you check your account, I sent you the credits."

"You can go fuck yourself."

Stilletta James turned and walked out. She was angry but wearing a smile. Gates was an asshole, but he believed her story.

TRACK 15

JOHN HENRY NEEDED TO GET back to Guru's to get a boombox antennae. It was the piece he needed to be able to shut down the bomb from a distance without Robert Graft IV knowing. He remembered seeing one back there when he was looking for the phone.

Martial law was still in effect and only a few Whites were being let across the Pigeon Line. Before Stilletta James had left to the police station, John Henry had made copies of her watch metadata and her Ox. Any robots he encountered would think he was her. It would work if he didn't come in contact with any Pigeon Pats.

He got on the subway and across the Pigeon Line. When he arrived, there was no one else on the train or in the station which put him on edge. He wanted to listen to music but thought it would be better he didn't so no one surprised him.

The walk to Guru's was a long one. The last time he walked this way he ended up beaten up in the Pigeon Police station. No one was around this time.

"They must all be around the police station," he thought to himself. The thought gave him comfort but didn't slow the thumping bass in his chest and ears. He soaked his SMiRK with nervous sweat. He only felt relief once he put his hand on the door to Guru's.

"Johnny Steel!" Gibran shouted as he saw John Henry enter the store. "You're alive!"

Gibran clapped him on the back and gave him a big hug. This was the most emotion John Henry had seen out of Gibran in all of their meetings.

"I thought they put your fire out for sure after what Stilletta James told me."

"Almost king," John Henry replied as he showed him his black arm.

"What happened?"

"Graft tried to mirk me. Sun got my arm before Stilletta found me and got me down."

"Does it hurt?" Gibran asked.

"Nah. It did at first. Felt like it was microwaved. But now nothing. I can't move it."

"Well I guess you're not as Black as I thought," Gibran said with a chuckle trying to lighten the mood. "Why were they fucking with you anyway?"

John Henry told him the story of why Robert Graft IV.

"He wants to bomb the sun away? That cat is washed for sure."

"Stilletta went to the police station to distract them so we could get a head start to stop him. I need to get a few things here before we head out."

John Henry and Gibran went to the back. The boombox was where he remembered it. He took out the remaining phones and went to work. It was hard doing things with one hand, but Gibran jumped in when he needed help. He was done by the time Stilletta James walked into the store.

"You ready king?" Stilletta James asked John Henry

"I think so." He had practiced turning things on with the phones but hadn't really spent much time with Robert Graft IV turning things off. It should work in theory, but he wasn't sure how much range he needed to have. "I don't know how close we'll have to get."

"Before you go, let me give you something for good luck."

Gibran went behind his counter where he kept his memorabilia and came back with a record sleeve in his hand.

"You want us to take a record?" John Henry asked with a quizzical expression.

"Nah king. *The* record," Gibran said as he pulled it out. It was a silver looking record with yellow in the middle. "This is one of the original platinum prints of Wu Tang Forever. Track 2 is Triumph. I figure you could use the swag."

John Henry just held the record in his hands. It was heavier than it looked, almost like a wheel of steel. As he was rotating it in his hands his eshirt flickered and lit up. The others looked at it too.

"What the fuck?" John Henry said out loud puzzled.

The shirt focused and it was a picture of Robert Graft IV. The pale white face and red eyes looking out. His mouth was moving but there was no sound.

"What's happening John Henry?" Stilletta James asked.

"I don't know."

Then words begin to flash.

"One. Hour. Before. Sun. Down. Power. To. The. Fathers."

Then the shirt went dark for a second. Then lit up with a timer.

"1:00" it read.

"Oh shit, we gotta find out where he is," John Henry said. He scrambled to pull out one of the phones and turned it on. Robert Graft IV had kept his phone off but now it was on to send this message out. They all looked at the map to locate the icon.

"Is that the old Graft Tower?" Gibran asked when he saw where the icon showed up. They all looked at the streets.

"Of course, it is," John Henry muttered.

"We'll have to take the subway, it's the only way to get there in time," Stilletta James said. "Let's go."

TRACK 16

THE PLATINUM ALBUM DIDN'T FIT in John Henry's backpack so instead he clipped it to the outside. It seemed absurd and conspicuous as they ran to the subway station, but Gibran wouldn't let them leave without it. John Henry and Stilletta James conceded when they realized arguing with him was going to just eat into the ticking time on John Henry's eshirt.

On the way, they passed several people. It looked like everyone received the same message and countdown from Robert Graft IV. Now it was the same ticking clock, a constant reminder of how little time they had to stop him.

John Henry did feel a little bit of pride that his innovation could reach out to everyone in the city. He thought about the possibilities in the future, if there was a future.

Stilletta James brought him back to reality.

"John Henry look at the station entrance, that's not normal right?" she asked. There were two Pigeon Police officers guarding the stairs down to the platform. The last couple of weeks made up the bulk of her subway experience, but it didn't feel right.

"Shit, the Pigeon Pats must be on alert because of the bombing and Graft's message."

Stilletta James paused and thought.

"Give me your backpack. You got any chords in here?" she finally said.

"For sure."

She took one out of the backpack.

"Put your hands behind your back and let me tie them up."

John Henry started to get nervous. He didn't like where her plan was going. One time in the Pigeon Police interrogation room was enough for him.

"Walk in front of me. Trust me, I got this," she assured him.

Stilletta James put John Henry's backpack on and pushed him forward just a little bit.

"Yo, chill with that," John Henry replied.

"I gotta make it look real, king. Don't get coaled up. Stay with me."

As they walked up to the station entrance, Stilletta James recognized the officers stationed at the top of the stairs. At least she wouldn't have to convince them who she was.

"What's up kings, how ya'll rollin'?" Stilletta James greeted them trying to keep it casual.

"It's crazy queen. Everyone's fired up. The City's on lock down. This countdown has people trippin'. Got us out here trying to maintain control. Who's the smirk?" one of the officers responded.

"Commander Gates had me tracking this smirk down," Stilletta James could feel John Henry's body stiffen as she said the slur, but she knew she had to sell it. "Caught him a few blocks down walking with this backpack."

"They're always trying to sneak over the Pigeon Line and steal something. Probably trying to loot now that everybody is locked down." As he said this, he hit John Henry in the face with the butt of his rifle and laughed. "Fucking smirk!"

It was Stilletta James' turn to bristle, but she couldn't dwell on it because she had to catch John Henry's body as stumbled toward her with his hands still tied.

He didn't let out a sound which surprised her, but under the hood of the SMiRK his teeth clenched.

The ringing in John Henry's ears drowned out what the police were saying. His coal was fired up, but he knew he couldn't do anything. They had to stop Robert Graft IV plus his hands were tied. He continued his silence as his head pulsed with pain again, reminding him the interrogation room visit wasn't so long ago.

"You guys want to take him in? Trying to get back home before this countdown stops. Who knows what's going to happen?"

"Nah queen. We got orders to stay at the station and watch for the Graft.

Cameras all over the City but we gotta watch this shit. Wrash task if you ask me."

"Alright then kings. I'll take him. Gates better have my money. Be steady."

The officers stepped aside as she guided John Henry down the stairs.

Once she was out of earshot from the officers, Stilletta James let her shoulders and back release and gave a sigh as she continued down the stairs.

"You okay?" she said in a low tone just to be careful.

"Fuck queen. They almost knocked me out. Was that part of your plan?" John Henry snapped in a whisper.

"Sorry king. I guess I should have seen that coming," she said. Stilletta James had seen officers do things like that before, but this was the first time she felt guilty about it, which made her feel even worse about it. Her dark skin hid the flush in her face.

John Henry shook his head again in attempt to clear the ringing in his ears. Then he looked at his watch.

"45 minutes left. We gotta get to Graft Tower."

They hurried on to the waiting subway train. John Henry slumped down on to the chair and leaned his head against the window.

John Henry spoke as the train lurched forward.

"Fuck, all I wanted was to be a rapper," he said as he leaned his head back against the subway car window.

"What did you think was going to happen? You were going to say some rhymes on the Black side of town and get them to care about the Wrash?"

He leaned forward and put his head in his good hand.

"I don't know. I think the whole time I thought maybe I *was* Black and I deserved to be heard. I had hip hop in my blood. My mom, maybe my dad. If only I could get out and prove it. But nah. Just a fucking White kid from the Wrash," he said as he nudged his dead arm forward at the shoulder.

"John Henry. Hip hop started out Black music no doubt. Its roots go way back when power was different. That doesn't mean you can't do it if you're White. You just gotta respect the culture. Give props to where it came from and not ignore it. It's bigger than hip hop."

John Henry leaned back again. He didn't talk for a minute or two.

"I think sometimes I just feel lost. Hip hop was my sun growing up. Something to lose myself in and shine a light into the abyss. I just wanted to be the ray in the darkness for others. Find my beat, where I fit into the rhythm."

"You just gotta take that sun and reflect it back to everyone else. It will show you the rhythm."

John Henry nodded his head and he thought about what he was looking for.

The train jerked to a stop and shook him from his thoughts. John Henry jumped up with an energy and bounce that Stilletta James didn't expect.

"Let's go!" he said and ran out.

TRACK 17

THE TIME SHOWED ONLY 20 minutes left. Graft tower was one block from the subway station. There were no officers at the station entrance. Like Graft Park nobody was in this part of the city. It was a deadzone.

They were out of breath when they reached the tower. The doors at the front were chained closed but the windows all around them were shattered. There was no sign of any other Graft at the tower. It looked like nobody had been there in years.

John Henry pulled out one of the phones and turned the screen on. The phone they were running to was still displayed at this location.

"He's still here."

The stepped through the jagged glass trying not to cut themselves. John Henry tugged on his SMiRK as it got caught on one of the shards.

The faded red carpet was frayed and matted. What furniture populated the lobby was turned on its side. The fading sun provided just enough light to see where the doors to the stairs were located.

Before going into the stairwell, John Henry pulled out the phone and extended telescoping antenna he had added at Guru's. He pressed the button on the screen, but nothing happened.

"We're still out of range," John Henry said. "He's gotta be in the penthouse. That's twenty stories up. C'mon."

John Henry turned on their flashlight and they both headed into the stairwell.

It was hard to see with just the flashlight, but they pounded up the stairs as fast as they could with a hand on the rail.

They had made it up ten stories. Their legs hurt and their hearts pounded in their chests.

Stilletta James put her hand on the wall.

"Check it!" Stilletta James said in between depth breaths.

John Henry made a motion and the screen of the phone lit up. The application he had made popped up. He pressed the screen and then looked at his watch. He pressed the screen a couple of times more and then back to the watch.

"Nothing queen. It's still going. We only have five minutes. We need to get closer."

John Henry couldn't make out Stilletta James face in the dark, but he could tell where her thoughts were. Questions they hadn't thought about in their rush to get to Graft Tower. Where was the bomb? Would Robert Graft IV blow himself up?

The silence and stillness lasted for a second before they both raced up the stairs again. Lungs still on fire, but they had to keep going.

At last they arrived at the final landing. John Henry still in full sprint mode went to open the door but slammed into it instead.

"Fuck! It's locked."

"Try it again!"

John Henry went back to the screen. As it lit up, he checked is watch.

"Only one-minute left."

John Henry hit the button he had tried earlier on the phone. Before he could check his watch, they both heard a loud yell. It came from the other side of the door but sounded far off and muted. He looked down at his watch. The timer had stopped.

"I think It worked."

They both slumped to the floor in relief and exhaustion. Stilletta James laid on her back. She hadn't run like that in a long time.

They continued to hear yelling on the other side of the door but couldn't make out the words.

"Graft is in there. He's probably all coaled up because you shut it down."

"We gotta check it out. The only way to stop him for sure is to get that last phone back."

"The doors locked though," Stilletta James lamented as she sat up.

"I think I can get it, turnaround so I can get into the backpack."

John Henry rifled through it for a second and then pulled out a small multi-tool. He pressed a button and a small electrical motor whirred and Stilletta James could see something move. He stuck it into the door frame. The sound changed tone as the small saw engaged with the door bolt. It took a few seconds, but John Henry made it through it. The door swung open as the smell of hot metal wafted in the air.

The yelling was still going on. Robert Graft IV hadn't heard them. They looked through the doorway into an empty lobby. It wasn't decrepit like the lobby. It looked like a snapshot of history with a muted layer of dust. The gilding on the tiles or the molding didn't hold a shine but wasn't rusted.

There were no signs of any other Graft members.

"Where is everybody?" Stilletta James whispered to John Henry.

He just shrugged his shoulders and continued into the penthouse. They both placed each step with care not to make a sound. They probably didn't need to be so careful with all the yelling they were hearing, but they were nervous and didn't want to give up the element of surprise.

They walked deeper into the penthouse. Both of them stopped next to the master bedroom door. It was open and there was light within. They couldn't see him, but it sounded like he was talking to someone. His tone was manic.

"Fuck! This fucking phone! It was working, why isn't it working?"

They could hear him slamming what must have been the phone on the counter.

Robert Graft IV went on.

"I'm just trying to make the world a better place. Make everyone equal again like it used to be. But nooo they can't have that. The Blacks want all the power to themselves. They took what the Fathers gave, and they ruined it! Grandaddy, they ruined it! I'm sorry I failed. I tried to be a patriot. I tried to show them the way. Give me liberty or give me death. But now everyone is dead. I'm the only one left. Robert and Jackson blew themselves up for freedom. For equality! Power to the Fathers! But now it's just me. And this fucking phone won't work. Piece of shit."

Something skidded across the floor and out of the door. John Henry and Stilletta James looked at each other and then looked down at the phone. John Henry leaned down to get it but stopped when he saw a shadow loom in the doorway.

They froze as they listened to his steps get closer and closer. His pale face appeared first. He had his green SMiRK on but wasn't wearing the hood. He bent down to pick up the phone, still not seeing Stilletta James and John Henry who were in the shadows but close enough to touch him. He turned around and walked back through the door.

They both gave a sigh of relief and looked at each other.

Before they could do anything, they heard a rustle followed by a click. A green arm held a gun around the door aiming their direction.

"Don't you even fucking move," they heard Robert Graft IV's voice as his body followed behind the arm and the gun out into the hallway. "Get in here!"

Robert Graft IV motioned the gun toward the room but kept it pointed at them.

"Just the person I wanted to see! You see, I'm sure you stopped my bomb. But now you can fix it! Grandad is going to be so proud of me. You see. Whites will have equality again. It will be just like the Fathers imagined it. Every man with life, liberty, and property! You see John Henry! I tried to tell you. We could have done it together. Imagine the world. Like it used to be! Now fix the fucking phone!" He fired a shot into the wall.

He tossed the phone to John Henry who caught it with one hand.

"What happened to your arm?" Robert Graft IV said with a chuckle. "Get a little sun?"

John Henry glared at him and looked down at his arm and then at the phone in his working hand. He didn't know what to do. Robert Graft IV wouldn't shoot him until he fixed the phone. He had to delay to buy time.

"Go on. Fix it," Robert Graft said motioning the gun to him.

"I'll try, but you were throwing it all over the place. It could be broken."

"I don't care if it's fucking broken. Do it with one of your other phones. I know you have more in the backpack," Robert Graft IV said as he shoved Stilletta James towards John Henry.

Stilletta James bit her tongue and glared at him.

"Get the phones and then she can back away."

John Henry tucked two phones under his dead arm and then Stilletta James backed away. John Henry started messing with one of the screens with his good hand. His SMiRK was still on and sweat was beading up on his face under the hood.

"Drop the fucking gun!" shouted a voice from the doorway.

Everyone's head turned to look at the door. Commander Gates stood there aiming his gun at Robert Graft IV. John Henry was in between the two and he stood their frozen.

"Aww *the* Commander Gates. I owe you a debt of gratitude. Without you, Whites would have been complacent years ago. Would have forgotten all about the founding fathers but no. You reminded them what inequality looks like. You gave us a purpose. Making everything right again."

"Cool it Graft. I came here to kill you. To end this."

The two men kept their guns trained on each other as they spoke.

"Don't you get it Gates? It will never end. You kill me. Someone just like me will spring up. Carry the banner of the Fathers. Their vision was too pure. You can't kill it."

"Maybe not but killing you will give me some satisfaction."

"You can try. But maybe you hit Johnny boy here instead. He worked so hard to get here to stop me. You gonna kill him too?"

John Henry looked at Commander Gates as he responded.

"You think I care about him? I thought you mirked him. If he dies, he'll be one less White hooligan on the streets."

Stilletta James couldn't believe what she was his hearing. His father willing to let him die.

Gates tightened his grip on his gun and aimed it at Robert Graft IV. John Henry stared back at him looking down the barrel of the gun. Stilletta James dove at John Henry.

"Die!!!" Robert Graft yelled in a high pitch scream and he pulled his trigger. So did Gates.

The record on the backpack shattered as Stilletta James and John Henry fell to the floor.

Both Gates and Graft let out screams and dropped their guns. Stilletta James rolled off of John Henry. Her heart was beating out of her chest and into her head. Adrenaline raced through her veins.

"Are you okay?" she asked John Henry.

He patted his hand all over his body checking for blood and a bullet hole. His adrenaline was racing too, and he was sure he should be shot somewhere. He had felt something hit his body before Stilletta James tackle him. Then he saw it and chuckled. Stilletta James shot him a quizzical look

"They got me," John Henry said as he pointed to his dead arm. A hole. He laughed some more.

"Thank god," Stilletta James let out with a sigh as she started to calm down.

They both sat up and looked around to see what happened to Commander Gates and Robert Graft IV who were both writhing in pain.

Robert Graft IV was rolling on the ground cradling his groin. The green SMiRK was soaked in blood where he was holding something metallic. In similar fashion, Commander Gates had his hands to his face tugging at a shiny object sticking from his eye.

They looked around and realized what had happened. A bullet from one of the guns had hit the record on the backpack. It exploded sending shards everywhere. One had hit Commander Gates in the eye, and another had wounded Graft below the waist.

Stilletta James helped John Henry up with his good arm.

"I guess Wu Tang Clan ain't nothing to fuck with," Stilletta James said.

"Queen, you corny."

They laughed as they walked out of the room rapping the rest of the song.

ACKNOWLEDGEMENTS

THIS STORY HAS BEEN A long time coming. I thought of the idea more than a decade ago and kept telling myself I would write it one day. I owe it to my wife, Whitney, who sometimes could see the passion I had for this more than I could. As she does, she pushed me to get comfortable with being uncomfortable and set goals and actually write it. I could not have written this book without her and her willingness to put our family on her back while I wrote my dreams. I'll always love and appreciate her for helping me unlock my potential and perspective in all things.

I want to give a shout out to my friends David Hakim and David Cuffeld. They were the first people to read this story who were not my wife. Their willingness to do so gave me hope that maybe I wasn't writing this story for only me, maybe somebody else *would* read it. I'll forever appreciate their time and their feedback.

I want to thank my family for encouraging me to be a writer, even when sometimes I know they were just saying it. My mom's mom goggles have always given me confidence, "like, yeah I can do this." My brother has always been there as a listening ear and a no-nonsense critic when I needed to hear it.

There are so many along my hip hop journey and education that I want to thank.

Thanks to my dad for giving me an MC Hammer cd for my birthday.

Thanks to my aunt Linda who let me buy the Wu Tang Forever album despite the parental advisory on the front.

Thanks to the homie Mushfik who let me cop his copy of Binary Star – Masters of the Universe. That shit changed my life for real.

Shout out to all my homies in Aldea who showed me what's up. Joven, you always challenge me to be better person, to think before I speak, not to mention putting me on to the Visionaries. Jon Doe, your turntables and love for hip hop were the soundtrack for my life for years. Pedro, you're like a brother to me and are always down to wax poetic. Seward, you would give the shirt off your back and probably have multiple times. It's been too long since we've all kicked it. I'm thinking Paid Dues 2005. Bring it back!

Kevin, Katrina, and Jeff. So many shows! Kevin thanks for getting me to go to the Coup and then meet Boots Riley even though I had a test the next day. Kevin and Katrina, Binary Star reunion! That weed brownie was lit! We survived though and then chilled with One Be Lo. Crazy. Jeff, watching Atmosphere do Shrapnel, so good.

Last, I just want to say that hip hop helped make me who I am today. Without this music and this culture, I would not have the personal creed and beliefs I do. So many styles and messages throughout but the theme that stands out for me the most is *knowledge of self*. Knowing who I am and what I'm about and the confidence and swagger to rep it with pride. This art has a lot to teach and I hope that maybe this book will set someone on a journey that I started back in the day but still goes strong.

www.ingramcontent.com/pod-product-compliance
Lightning Source LLC
Chambersburg PA
CBHW020623130626
46552CB00003B/1082